THE SPIDER:
THE SPIDER AND THE PAIN MASTER

MASTER OF MEN!

THE SPIDER AND THE PAIN MASTER

By Grant Stockbridge

POPULAR PUBLICATIONS • 2024

CHAPTER 1
THE SPIDER'S ON THE WAY!

IN A room on the ninth floor of the Mallard Hotel, over-looking Times Square, a frightened man sat tense and watchful. He was facing the door, and his eyes seemed to be glued to the knob, waiting for it to turn.

There were beads of sweat on his forehead. Every few minutes he would run a hairy hand over his heavy jowls. But it was always his left hand. The right never moved, for it kept a heavy automatic pistol trained unwaveringly upon the door.

On the floor were two cowhide bags, all packed and ready for him to check out. A tan overcoat and a tan fedora lay on the bed. The coat was an expensive one, and so was the hat. The man's suit was of the best, and the cowhide bags were the finest that money could buy.

Yet their owner was not happy. He was frightened. His fear was apparent in the close-set, smallish eyes, and in the occasional twitch of his thick lips. His eyes never left the door knob. He sat there that way for perhaps fifteen minutes, and then the telephone rang.

The frightened man uttered a gasp of relief. But he did not remove his gaze from the door. He reached over without shifting position, and picked up the telephone handset on the night table alongside the bed.

"Yes?" he said into the instrument, almost in a whisper.

Scimitars flashed... but the
Spider's guns were barking.

"Sabin?" a cold, unemotional voice asked. "Yes. This is Sabin."

"Are you ready?"

"Yes, I'm ready."

"Very well. Wait exactly fifteen minutes. It will then be nine-fifteen. Call a bell boy and have your bags taken downstairs. Pay your bill. That should take ten minutes, bringing it to nine-twenty-five. After you pay your bill, stop and buy cigarettes or a newspaper. You will then walk out of the front entrance at exactly nine-thirty by the clock in the hotel lobby. The doorman will offer to get you a cab, but you will refuse. At exactly that moment, an Onyx taxicab will cruise past. You will flag that cab and get into it with your bags. Do you understand?"

"Yes. I understand."

"All right. Set your watch at nine-ten, when you hear the signal. Goodbye—"

"Wait!" Sabin exclaimed hoarsely. "There's—there's something I have to tell you!"

"Well?" demanded the unemotional voice at the other end. "Speak quickly. Otherwise you will upset the schedule."

"It—it's about the—the Spider!"

"What!" The cold voice lost a little of its evenness. "What about the Spider?"

"He—he called up. He said he knew who I was. He said I'll never leave the country alive. He said he's coming here to get me. I tell you," Sabin's voice rose to a shrill, high-pitched key, *"he's on his way here!"*

There was a momentary pause at the other end. Then the voice said, "I see. It is good that you have told me this. Everything

4

shall be taken care of. You will proceed according to schedule. *We* will handle the Spider!"

"But—but can you get here in time? He may be already in the hotel!"

"Have no fear, Sabin. My men are there now. They will see to it that the Spider ceases to annoy us!"

There was a click. The phone went dead.

Sabin hung up. His face was broken out in perspiration. But all during the talk he had never removed his gaze from the door, nor had his gun wavered.

He licked his lips, and kept on watching the knob….

NINE FLOORS below, in the lobby of the Mallard Hotel, a man in a black overcoat and a black fedora sat in one of the public phone booths. He was not using the phone, however. He was watching all who came and went in the lobby—and he was waiting for a call.

When the phone rang, he snatched the receiver off the hook quickly. Strangely, the phone did not ring very loud. It made only a faint tinkle which was barely audible beyond the booth. The man in the black fedora put his lips to the mouthpiece and said, "Thirteen."

A cold, unhurried voice at the other end said, "Seven."

The man in the black hat whispered, "Twenty-six. This is Loder."

"Emergency!" rapped the voice at the other end. "The Spider is coming for Sabin. He will try to enter the hotel, or he is already there. Take all precautions to prevent his reaching Sabin. Cover all exits. *The Spider must not escape!* That is all."

The phone clicked dead.

Loder swore softly under his breath. He replaced the receiver, and hurried out of the phone booth. A thin man with a flat nose was sitting in the lobby, facing the desk and reading a newspaper. Loder passed close to this man, and stopped to light a cigarette. Out of the corner of his mouth he said, "Emergency. Spider coming—or already here. See that the back entrance is covered."

The man with the flat nose only rustled his paper in response. He waited until Loder had passed on, then he got up and walked to the rear of the lobby. There was a side street entrance here. He stepped out into the street and walked ten paces in the shadow of the building. He stopped alongside the alley between the hotel and the theatre next door. There was apparently no one in that alley. But the man with the flat nose spoke as if he were talking to thin air.

"Thirteen," he said.

From somewhere in the alley came the response, "Seven."

"Emergency," said the man with the flat nose. "The Spider is coming—or is already here. Cover this exit. Spread the word to all men posted here. We'll trap the Spider tonight."

He did not wait for a reply. He turned and reentered the hotel, resuming his chair in the lobby. He opened up his paper, and held it in front of him with his left hand, as if he were reading. With his right he took a revolver from a shoulder holster, and held it in his lap, concealed by the newspaper. He looked across to the telephone booth. Loder was inside it again. He nodded to Loder, who nodded imperceptibly in reply.

The phone in the booth rang again. Once more Loder picked it up and said, "Thirteen."

Once more that cold, unemotional voice said, "Seven."

"Twenty-six," said Loder. "Loder speaking again. All arrangements made, Bragg has just passed the word. If the Spider comes, it will be impossible for him to escape."

"Very good," said the cold voice. "Sabin is leaving on schedule. Have you seen anyone enter who might be the Spider?"

"No," Loder said. "I have my eye on the entrance. The only one who came in was that Wentworth fellow, you know, the rich polo player. He had his fiancée with him, Nita van Sloan. Their pictures are always on the society page. Wentworth and the van Sloan girl went into the cocktail lounge."

"Wentworth, eh!" said the voice, speculatively. "He is a friend of Commissioner Kirkpatrick. I wonder… perhaps you had better check on him, Loder. See if he's still in there."

"Right," said Loder.

He hung up and left the booth. He started across the lobby, and when he came abreast of the chair in which the flat-nosed man was sitting, he looked down at his feet and frowned. He stooped, and went through the motions of tying his shoelace. He spoke out of the corner of his mouth.

"Go in the cocktail lounge," he said. "Richard Wentworth is in there, with Nita van Sloan. Keep your eye on Wentworth. Red Feather has an idea he may be the Spider."

"Right," said the flat-nosed man.

Loder fixed his shoelace, got up and returned to the phone booth. The flat-nosed man put his gun in his side coat pocket, folded the newspaper, and arose. He strolled casually toward the cocktail lounge....

IN THE cocktail lounge, Richard Wentworth and Nita van Sloan were sipping dry Martinis, and reading a newspaper which was spread out on the bar in front of them. It was the same edition that the flat-nosed man in the lobby had been holding. The headline was black, and still damp:

RED FEATHER STRIKES AGAIN!
LAURA BURGESS BURNED TO DEATH BY GHASTLY
FLAMETHROWERS AS SHE STEPS FROM TAXICAB!
Heron's Feather, Dyed in Human Blood, is Left Beside Charred and
Blackened Body of Famous Actress!

Nita van Sloan's beautifully chiseled, patrician face was white with emotion. Her long, slender hands were clenched in her lap.

"Lord, Dick!" she breathed through pallid lips, "I knew Laura Burgess!" She closed her eyes as if to shut out a terrible vision. "Laura—burned to death! She was so beautiful and so talented! Who... who could have wanted to destroy her... and *why?*"

Richard Wentworth's eyes were grim. "The man who calls himself Red Feather; the man who leaves the grisly token beside the bodies of his victims—a feather dipped in human blood! Red Feather is like an octopus that has spread his tentacles out to tear at the nerves of people in all walks of life!"

Wentworth's voice dropped an octave, and his eyes took on

8

that faraway look which Nita knew so well. "Red Feather has a terrible advantage over any other criminal I have ever encountered. He is absolutely without a sense of mercy. In some secret way he has managed to batter down the resistance of good and decent people to the point where he can force them to do vile things. *He must be stopped!*"

Nita, seeing the faraway look in his eyes, and hearing his words, drew in her breath sharply. "Dick! You—you're going to—"

She sighed, seeing the grim resolve upon his face.

"Yes, darling," he said slowly. "The Spider is going to walk again tonight! Before morning, I hope to learn the identity of Red Feather!"

"You've been holding out on me, Dick!" she said breathlessly. "You had a purpose in coming here?"

"Yes, darling. A little private information." His finger slid down the page, indicating a small item at the bottom:

ARNOLD METZ STILL MISSING
Alleged Absconder Believed to be in
Hiding Somewhere in New York

It was discovered today that Arnold Metz, missing bank president, was two hundred thousand dollars short in his accounts. It is believed...

"Arnold Metz," he told her, "is right here in the Mallard Hotel. He's registered under the name of Sabin."

Nita frowned, looking at the news item. "But I don't understand. What has Metz to do with Red Feather?"

"For some reason which I haven't yet discovered, Metz stole that money to give to Red Feather. He's to turn it over tonight, and Red Feather will help him to leave the country. I've made arrangements to… er… pay a little call on Metz before he leaves. He has already been warned that the Spider is coming for him!"

Nita's eyes opened wide with consternation. "Then Red Feather knows it too! He'll trap you—"

Wentworth smiled tightly. "I am hoping he will make the attempt!"

From his pocket he took a small vial which he slipped into her hand. "If there should be trouble, you know what to do with this. I'm going now. If anyone follows me out of here, try to detain him for three or four minutes. That is all the time I'll need for a start."

He arose from his chair, and looked at his wrist watch. Then, raising his voice for the benefit of anyone who might be listening: "I'll just go around and pick up those opera tickets for tomorrow, Nita. It's only around the corner. I shan't be gone long," and under his breath he added, *"I hope!"*

She smiled the smile that meant much more than: "Good luck, Dick."

She turned around in her chair, and watched Wentworth's lithe and powerful figure as he moved toward the street entrance of the cocktail lounge. At the same moment, she saw a man enter the lounge from the hotel lobby. He was a burly man with a flat nose which looked as if it had been smashed at one time by a battering-ram.

Nita's glance flicked over this man, and she noted that his gaze was on Wentworth. When he saw that Dick was going out into the street, he immediately swerved and turned to follow him.

NITA VAN SLOAN grew tense. Wentworth must not be followed now. Within the next few moments he was going to transform himself into the Spider. He must be left free and unobserved.

Desperately, Nita sought some means to keep the flat-nosed man there.

Wentworth was already through the doorway, and the man was halfway along the bar, toward the door. Nita's eyes glinted. She got off the chair, holding her cocktail glass.

"Mr. Smith!" she called out sharply.

Nita van Sloan might have given the average observer the impression that she was a carefree society girl with plenty of looks and plenty of sex appeal, but not too much brains. That impression would have been highly erroneous. For behind those warm violet eyes there ticked a brain which was a match for that of the cleverest of men. Less than that would have failed to make her a fitting mate for Richard Wentworth. Her native intelligence and quick-witted grasp of the most abstruse problems had been augmented by the things Wentworth had taught her. Among them was a sound knowledge of practical psychology, gleaned not only from the works of world-renowned experts, but also from actual experiments in the finely equipped psychological laboratory maintained by Wentworth. One of the experiments they had tried was that of calling a common name in a high, sharp voice. Tests had proved conclusively that forty-eight people out of fifty will turn around involuntarily, even though their own name has not been called, because curiosity is one of the strongest of human instincts.

This time, the flat-nosed man reacted true to form. His eyes had been glued to Wentworth's back. But when Nita sang out: *"Mr. Smith!"* he turned around.

Nita hurried over to him, carrying her cocktail, and smiling with apparent pleasure.

"Why, Mr. Smith!" she exclaimed, extending her hand, which he could not help taking. "Imagine meeting you here! I thought you would be in Monte Carlo at this time of the year!"

The flat-nosed man frowned. "I'm afraid you've made a mistake, madam. My name is not Smith—"

"What!" Nita's face fell, in a beautiful registration of amazement. "You're not Lorenzo Smith, the painter?"

"I'm sorry, madam, but that is not my name. If you will excuse me—"

"Oh," she said contritely. "I'm so sorry. I was sure you were Lorenzo Smith. Do you know, you would very easily pass for his double?"

"Very interesting, I'm sure," the man said. "And now, if you will excuse me, I'm in a bit of a hurry—"

He tried to release his hand from hers, but she clung to it.

12

"You know," she said, "I very seldom forget a face. Are you sure you weren't in Monte Carlo three years ago?"

"I have never been in Monte Carlo in my life, madam!" he said bitingly. "And my name is not Smith. Goodbye, madam!"

Reluctantly, Nita released his hand. "Well, goodbye and—oh, I'm so sorry!" She made a deliberately awkward gesture, and spilled the contents of her Martini glass down the front of his coat.

Flat Nose jumped back, with his face twisted in a scowl.

Nita uttered a little gasp of dismay. "Oh, how stupid of me!"

She put down her glass, and snatched the handkerchief which Flat Nose had taken from his pocket. "Let me dry it for you."

"It's all right," he said hastily, but still scowling. "It'll dry by itself. I have to be going—"

"Oh, I wouldn't think of letting you go like that! It was my entire fault. Here, it will only take a moment."

She held on to his coat, and dabbed at the stain.

Mr. Flat Nose growled. "I told you I was in a hurry!" He yanked the handkerchief out of her hand, glared at her, and hurried into the street.

Nita van Sloan watched him go, with a little secret smile. She had held him up long enough for Wentworth to lose him. She turned and winked to the bartender. "Another martini, Thomas. I really don't know *how* I could have been so awkward!"

CHAPTER 2
THE SPIDER RIDES THE WEB

UP ON the ninth floor, the man who was registered as Mr. Sabin was still in his chair facing the door, with the black automatic in his hand. He kept looking constantly at his watch. There were still seven minutes to go before he could call for a bellboy.

That door—it was the only way the Spider could reach him. The window behind him was locked, and the shade was drawn all the way down. There were no fire escapes, and no terraces on this fireproof hotel. Not even a fly could walk nine floors up the smooth face of the building. Neither could a fly walk down eleven floors from the roof.

But maybe… maybe… They told strange tales about the Spider, how he appeared from nowhere….

Suddenly Sabin jerked up out of his chair and swiveled around in a half crouch. The hand that held the gun started to shake as he stared at the shaded window. His whole body broke out in a cold sweat.

Distinctly he had heard it—somebody had tapped upon the window pane!

"God!" he muttered. "It—it *can't* be!"

He had to know. He had to be sure. Perhaps, in his overwrought condition, he had allowed his ears to deceive him. He must look. He must look out there and make sure it wasn't the Spider who had tapped.

A cunning look came into his eyes. He backed over to the

14

dresser and pushed it squarely in front of the door. That would keep anyone from entering that way. Then he reached out and flicked off the light switch. The room became utterly dark.

In the blackness, Sabin stole across the room, fingered the shade. He pulled it aside an inch, so that he could peer out.

He saw nothing.

Rendered a little bolder now, he pulled the shade all the way up, and opened the window. Still with his gun in his fist, he leaned out, peered above and below, and to both sides. There was nothing on the wall of the building. But someone had certainly tapped on the windowpane. To the right, the window of his own bathroom, adjoining his room, was dark. So was the window to the left of his room.

He shrugged. His nerves were going. He'd better get out of here. Probably almost time to call for a bellboy, anyway. He pulled in his head and closed the window, then pulled down the shade once more. Then he felt his way along the wall to the light switch and flicked it on. He still kept his gun gripped tightly, with finger on trigger, as the light sprang on. He blinked, and looked at the dresser. It was in place. No one had entered that way....

His eyes swiveled across the room to the bathroom doorway—and he uttered a shrill and terrible scream.

An utterly frightful figure was coming slowly out of the bathroom. Sabin recognized that low brimmed slouch hat, the voluminous black cape. It was the grisly death's head of a face which men had come to know as the fighting face of—the Spider! And in each of the Spider's hands was a long barreled revolver. Slowly, with dreadful, inexorable step, the Spider came toward him. And words came from those grim and frightful lips.

"Sabin, I have come for you—as promised. If you wish to live throw down your gun!"

SABIN'S FRIGHT was that of a cornered rat. He stood tensed and crouched, with the automatic thrust out at arm's length, his finger taut on the trigger.

"Damn you, Spider," he spat out, "don't come near me."

A queer and ominous laugh came from the cloaked figure. Slowly, the Spider advanced into the room. The two guns were at his hips, held low, but pointing at Sabin. And with each step he took, Sabin's fear increased.

"Well, Sabin," he said mockingly, "why don't you shoot? All you have to do is pull the trigger. Think of it, Sabin. You can pull that trigger, and shoot the Spider! Surely you would like to kill the Spider!"

Sabin's hand began to shake. He knew why the Spider was mocking him. Of course he could shoot and kill the Spider. But he knew that the moment he pulled his own trigger, those two

RICHARD WENTWORTH •

deadly guns in the Spider's hands would belch and vomit death. The Spider might die—but he, Sabin, would also die.

He backed away from the terrible, cloaked figure until he touched the wall. He could retreat no farther. The Spider was four feet away—three feet—two feet—then....

Sabin screamed in fright and rage, and fired!

But it was as if the ominous cloaked figure had read his mind, had timed his reactions to the last split-second of infinity. For just before Sabin pulled that trigger, the Spider's right gun flashed up and down with the speed of light. The long barrel cracked down hard upon Sabin's wrist, and the automatic exploded into the floor.

The gun blasted loudly in the close confines of the suite, and the thud it made when it dropped to the carpet from his numbed hand was drowned by the echoing reverberations of the shot.

Sabin cowered, defenseless, before the grim man whom the underworld feared more than the law—even more than death itself.

"Talk quickly, Sabin," the Spider said. "Who is helping you to escape from the country?"

"I—I'll talk, Spider. Red Feather—it's Red Feather who's helping me—"

"I know that. *Who is Red Feather?*"

"God help me, I don't know."

"Why did you steal from your bank? You didn't need the money."

"Red Feather made me do it."

"He forced you?"

"Yes."

"How?"

Sabin's lips trembled. "For the love of God, Spider, don't make me tell that. You don't know what you're doing—"

The Spider motioned impatiently. "Where is the money you stole?"

"In these two bags."

"How were you going to escape?"

"I'm to go downstairs and take an Onyx cab. That's all I know—except that they will get me out of the country by plane."

There was the sound of hurrying feet in the corridor. Men were coming to investigate the revolver shot.

"Sorry to do this, Metz. It's necessary!" One of the black gloved fists stabbed upward to Metz's chin, with the speed of a flying meteor. There was a thud, and Metz collapsed.

The cloaked figure of the Spider stooped and seemed to envelop him in the folds of the voluminous, purple lined cape. He was lifted bodily, apparently with the greatest of ease. The light switch was clicked off. In the abrupt darkness, a vague shadow moved through the room.

Somewhere nearby, a church bell tolled the quarter-hour. It was nine-fifteen—the time when the man who was known as Sabin should have called for a bellboy. But no call came down from room 913....

WHILE MEN continued to pound ineffectually at the door, the ephemeral shadow moved in the darkness with its burden, over to the window. The shade rasped as it was pulled upward. The window slid open, propelled by an almost invisible hand.

The darkness outside was only a little less opaque than within the room. Light waves from electric signs in the street below cast an eerie incandescence upon the side of the hotel. The window faced west, away from Broadway, over a low, three-story building next door. Beyond the low building was a taller structure—an old apartment house which had been converted to accommodate roomers. And from a window in that building, level with the tenth floor of the Mallard Hotel, a thin gossamer thread seemed to be stretched.

The shadowy figure of the Spider leaned out with its burden. There was another gossamer line hanging down from the tenth floor window, directly in front of the room Metz had engaged. The Spider grasped this line, and tied it around the body of the unconscious man. Then, while those in the corridor pounded at the door and shouted for it to be opened, the Spider picked up the two cowhide bags, and tied them also, with an extra loop, to the body of Metz.

So thin and frail did that line look that it seemed impossible that it could lift the combined weight of Metz and his two bags. Yet, when the Spider leaned out and uttered a low, peculiarly pitched whistle, the line began to rise, dragging the weight up from the floor and over the window sill. Slowly, surely, it swung out. For a moment Metz's unconscious figure dangled precariously in the air, with a drop of at least six flights to the roof below. The line tautened, but did not give.

This was the Spider's Web—a line of cleverly fabricated silken rope, cunningly made and treated with chemicals so that its tensile strength was as great as that of a ship's hawser.

As it started to rise, pulled slowly up by someone in the tenth floor window, the Spider seized it just above where it was tied around Metz's drooping body, and pushed himself out of the window. He wound his arm once around the line, leaving his other hand free, and hung, with his legs dangling in space. To anyone who might have looked in this direction from an adjoining building, little would have been visible except a vague mass swaying in the air, for the great black cape of the Spider covered Metz and the bags with a mantle of dark camouflage.

The Spider reached over and lowered the window, thus muffling the shouts of the men in the corridor outside the door. Then, while still hanging thus, he took from his pocket a long, thin, flexible tool with two prongs at one end. He inserted it in the crack between the upper and lower frames of the window, and then manipulated the prongs by means of a lever at the other end. This lever actuated the prongs through the medium of a powerful spring, so that they caught the window catch just like two human fingers. In a moment the window was locked. Now, those who entered the room would be faced with a puzzling problem. How had the Spider taken Metz out of there, with the doors and windows locked?

On entering through the bathroom, the Spider had previously locked the window. So that now there was no apparent way by which he could possibly have left the suite.

With the window locked, the Spider slipped the pronged tool out and put it away. Then he gripped the Web with both hands and whistled once more. Immediately the line began to rise.

From Metz's room came the sounds of breaking wood as those in the hall began to smash down the door.

The door was giving very fast now, and once they had it open, the dresser in front of it would present no obstacle. When those men entered the room, their first concern would be the window. They would surely see the great black shadow on the line outside, and then their guns would speak. It would be the end of the Spider.

BUT NO matter what the urgency, the Web could not move any faster. The Spider did not whistle again, for he knew that the one man up there on the tenth floor was exerting every ounce of his strength to pull him up. There was no use trying to hurry him.

Grimly, the Spider brought out one of his automatics. To trap him like this would indeed be a triumph for Red Feather's agents. But at least one of them would go to his death with the shadowy nemesis of crime!

Inch by inch the Web moved upward. Wood was splintering, inside the room, under the powerful blows of a fire axe. And suddenly, with a tremendous crash, the door gave inward. From where he hung on the line, the Spider could hear the dresser scraping along the floor as it was pushed back. Then he heard the rush of men into the room, and saw light stream through the window as they clicked on the switch.

The Spider was almost within reach of the upper window now. He put away the automatic, and stretched his free hand up toward the sill. But there was still a good six inches between the tips of his straining fingers and the safety of that ledge.

Below him, he heard the astounded shouts of men as they found room 913 empty.

"The window!" someone shouted. "He must have gone out the window—"

And another voice: "Nuts! How could he? The window's locked!"

While they were arguing, the Web moved up another few

inches. The Spider tried to help the man above, by bracing his feet against the wall. He could feel the tautness of the straining line, which was stretched rigid by the combined weight of himself, Metz and the two cowhide bags.

"What the devil!" someone in the room below was shouting. "We know he didn't come out through the door. So it *must* be the window. Let's look, anyway!"

The sash was raised, and a head poked out.

And just then, the Spider came within reach of the upper sill!

But it was too late. Looking down, he could see that the man at the window was peering toward the roof below. In a moment he would look up. That moment would seal the Spider's fate, for the man at the window down there was the house detective, and he had a gun in his hand.

The thought reactions of the Spider were lightning swift. Too many criminals had found that out to their sorrow. And now he was to demonstrate that speed of thought once more.

With the resourcefulness of one who has taught himself by rigid training to meet the swiftest emergency with swift action, he drew one of his automatics. But he did not fire it at the man below. That would not only have meant the killing of one who was probably an innocent party to the murderous designs of Red Feather—it would also have meant that those other men in the room would swarm to the window and send a blasting barrage of lead upward. And it would also have meant the failure of the Spider's plan to spirit Metz out from under the noses of Red Feather's organization.

So instead of shooting, the Spider sent his automatic spinning out through the darkness toward the roof below. He threw it just two seconds before the house detective began to turn his head upward, so that the man did not catch the flash of metal as it sped downward at a wide angle, over to the *left*. The Spider had seen the gun in the man's right hand. Knowing then that the detective was right-handed, he was able to tell which way he would turn his head when he was ready to look up. Long and interesting tests in the New York Laboratory of Psychological Research, endowed indirectly by the Spider, were constantly being conducted to ascertain and catalogue the normal reactions of human beings under any given set of circumstances. And one of those tests had proved conclusively that a right-handed man will turn his head to the right, while a left-handed man will turn his head to the left, when he looks around.

Thus, when the Spider threw that gun out toward the *left*, it was just at the moment when the house detective in the window below was turning his head toward the right, in order to look upward. So he did not notice the hurtling automatic. A second-and-a-half later, the weapon struck the roof below. Wentworth had slipped off the safety catch before hurling it, so that when it hit, the gun exploded thunderously.

THE SPIDER'S timing was uncannily accurate. Just at the moment when the detective's head was halfway around, the gun blasted below him. At once, he jerked his head back, peering down in the direction of the shot.

"Down there!" he yelled. "Someone's down there! I can't see him—"

He yanked his head in, and shouted to the others in Metz's

room, "He must have climbed down a rope ladder. He's on that lower roof! Come on! Let's go!"

In a moment those men were trooping out of the room, eager to be in the chase. And against the wall just above room 913, the Spider laughed harshly and gripped the sill above him. In a moment he had climbed over, and into the room.

A sturdy man with a military bearing was straining every muscle of his body as he hauled at the Web. He had his feet braced against the wall, and the coils of the line wrapped around his forearms, which were encased in leather cuffs. It was he who had been pulling that heavy load up to the tenth floor.

"Thank God, Major!" the man gasped as the Spider vaulted into the room beside him. "I heard those men below. I never thought I'd get you up in time!"

The Spider wasted no words. He swung to his feet, reached over the sill, and hauled at the unconscious body of Metz, which was still dangling outside. In a moment he had both Metz and the bags in the room.

"Good work, Jackson!" he complimented.

"Thank you, sir. What next?"

It was typical of this man that he engaged in no long-winded talk about the situation or its dangers, or about the almost super-human strength he had been compelled to exert for those few minutes when he hauled four hundred pounds of freight up one floor along the hotel wall.

That was just like Jackson. Those who saw him in normal life never gave him a second look. For his ostensible position was that of chauffeur to a wealthy polo player and sportsman by the

Hand over hand he crossed, high

above the surrounding roofs...

name of Richard Wentworth. Few people knew that Jackson had served as sergeant under Major Wentworth through long years of adventurous warfare in all parts of the world. And *none* knew that Jackson was the Spider's trusted aide at such times as these, when the Spider's life hung literally by a thread.

"We have less than six minutes, Jackson!" the Spider said as he lowered Metz to the floor. "It'll take them that long to get downstairs and around the corner. We will proceed as planned!"

As he talked, he leaned out of the window and tested the second Web line, which was looped around the steam radiator and went straight out across the low roof intervening, to the ninth floor window of the rooming house beyond. The line was taut. The Spider had come across on that only a few minutes ago, and now he was about to make the return journey with extra weight—and as Richard Wentworth, sportsman and millionaire. He removed the Spider costume and consigned it to Jackson.

Jackson was already ripping open the cowhide bags, using a keen edged knife. Money rumbled out of those bags—fives, tens, fifties, hundreds; bright crisp United States banknotes, and old wrinkled ones, all neatly banded, with the number of bills in each package plainly stamped on the bands. At a quick estimate there might have been two hundred thousand dollars in those two bags.

All this money, Jackson stuffed into a capacious black rubber sack. And while he did this, Wentworth was hooking a safety belt about his own waist. It was such a belt as a window washer might use on skyscrapers, but constructed of leather much wider and thicker. There was a hook at the side, and Wentworth stooped and lifted Metz's body and hooked it to the belt by the line of Web which was tied around Metz's waist. The inert body dangled, doubled over, as Wentworth straightened.

There was no lost motion on the part of either of those two men now. Jackson handed him the rubber bag, which he fastened to his belt thus leaving both hands free.

Jackson was now holding a stopwatch which had been on the floor. He glanced at it and said briefly, "One minute elapsed, sir."

Richard Wentworth nodded. "Five minutes left to get across! See you later, Jackson!"

"Goodbye, sir, and good luck!"

THE LITHE figure put a leg over the window sill, gripped the taut line in gloved hands, and swung free, hanging by his two hands. Then, swinging his body in bold, rhythmic strokes, he began to travel along the line, with the weight of Metz's inert body dragging at his belt.

The Web bowed under the weight, like a bowstring, but Wentworth never faltered. Hand over hand; he crossed, high above the low roof, toward the window of the rooming house beyond.

And behind him, Jackson hurried to a closet, coming back at once with a long Enfield sniper's rifle equipped with telescopic sights. Jackson knelt at the window, the rifle at his shoulder, his eyes fixed upon the roof above which his master was crossing. If anyone should emerge upon that roof while Wentworth was engaged in that aerial journey, and attempt to shoot him down, Jackson knew what to do.

Wentworth never once looked below him. His confidence

in Jackson was supreme. He bent all his energies to reaching that other window within the allotted span of five minutes. The going was hard, even for the superb muscles of Dick Wentworth. The strain upon him was terrific. But he did not flounder, or stop. Grimly, purposefully, he made his way across. It was only three and a half minutes by Jackson's stopwatch when he finally climbed over the sill of the rooming house window, and deposited his burden on the floor.

At once he signaled across, and Jackson loosened the loop of the Web from the radiator, allowing it to drop. At the other end Wentworth reeled in swiftly. Then Jackson took the two cowhide bags and heaved them out of the window. They landed with a crash on the roof below, and a moment later a skylight down there was thrust open. The house detective from the hotel pushed up on to the roof, and stopped to scratch his head over the two bags. Looking up, he saw no telltale sign of what had transpired. There was no light in that tenth floor window of the hotel, nor was there a light in the room into which Wentworth had disappeared.

Intently Wentworth leaned over Metz, whose unconscious body he had placed on the bed. The absconder was beginning to stir. Wentworth produced a small hypodermic. He drew off Metz's coat, and rolled up the sleeve of his shirt. Then he thrust the hypo needle into the man's arm, and pressed the plunger home. That hypo contained a dose of anesthetic which would keep Metz unconscious for at least seven hours.

The sack of money was stuffed into a laundry bag in the closet. Then, satisfied that everything was in order, Wentworth let himself out and took the self-service elevator down to the street floor. As he emerged from the hotel, he noted the crowd gathered at the entrance of the small building next door. But he passed right by them without displaying any interest, and reentered the Mallard Hotel through the street entrance....

CHAPTER 3
THE SPIDER GAS

IN THE cocktail lounge, Nita van Sloan tried to appear cool. She nibbled at the olive from her martini and engaged the barman in light conversation, designed to hide her anxiety. Constantly, her eyes kept flicking to her wrist watch. The time was dragging. It seemed to be hours—yet it was only six minutes since Wentworth had left.

A tall, extremely slender man entered the bar from the street entrance. His appearance immediately struck her like a blow in the face. She had never seen eyes so pitch-black, nor lips so thin and bloodless. The man's face was gaunt, almost skeletal. Yet there was an evil sort of attraction about him, which caught and held her fascinated attention.

The man came up to the bar, and the bartender greeted him with a sort of breathless respect.

"Good evening, Baron Crispi."

The man acknowledged the greeting negligently.

"Grand Marnier brandy, Thomas," he said, "with a drop of vermouth." His voice was cold, and absolutely expressionless.

Nita shuddered at the thought that this was an automaton speaking, and not a human being.

The Baron sipped his brandy-and-vermouth without even looking at her. Four minutes passed. There was a slight commotion out in the lobby, and the house detective came hurrying past. He stopped for a moment and whispered to Thomas at the end of the bar, and then went quickly to the elevator.

When Thomas came down and wiped her end of the bar, Nita asked him, "Anything wrong?"

"No, Miss van Sloan," he said. "I don't think so. One of the guests phoned down from the ninth floor that she thought she had heard a revolver shot. But so many people mistake backfire for gunshots—especially out-of-towners."

Nita strove to hide her anxiety. She gripped the stem of her glass, but did not move. Baron Crispi finished off his brandy quickly. There was still no expression in his face, as he hastily laid down a dollar bill. "Keep the change," he said, and went out into the lobby. He crossed to one of a row of phone booths. Loder was still sitting in the end one.

A moment after Baron Crispi had entered the middle one, Loder's phone rang with a musical tinkle. He took off the receiver, and said, "Thirteen."

"YOU FOOL!" said the cold, emotionless voice, dispensing this time with the balance of the identification code. "Where are all your men? The Spider has reached Sabin—under your very noses!"

"Impossible!" Loder said. "I have a man on the eighth floor, and a man on the tenth. No one could reach the ninth by the stairs. And I've got my eye on the elevators all the time. No cage has stopped at the ninth since you called."

"Never mind. The Spider has outwitted you somehow. But he's still in the hotel. He must not be allowed to escape. Are you sure every exit is covered?"

"Absolutely. We have twenty men operating here."

"Very well. Wentworth is your man.

He has left the cocktail lounge. The van Sloan girl is alone in there. Spread the word to watch for Wentworth. He is to be burned on sight."

"But—but supposing you're wrong? Suppose Wentworth is not the Spider?"

"That," the cold voice said, "is too bad for Mr. Wentworth. We shall give *ourselves* the benefit of the doubt. Goodbye!" The phone clicked dead, and Loder hung up. He left the booth just as the flat-nosed Blagg came into the lobby from the street.

"Pardon me," Loder said. "Have you got a light?"

Blagg took out a book of matches and struck a light. The first match didn't take, and it required another. This gave them extra time to exchange information.

"Did you check on Wentworth?" Loder asked, scarcely moving his lips.

"No, damn him! That van Sloan girl was too clever. She detained me for almost four minutes. When I got out to the street, he was gone. I've been snooping around the building, making sure that all the men are posted, and inquiring if they saw him."

"Did they see him?"

"No."

Loder finally got his light. "Red Feather just called. He's sure that Wentworth is the Spider. Orders are to kill Wentworth. Use two vacuum cleaners."

"Check," said Blagg. He left Loder, and crossed the lobby, disappearing out through the side street exit.

Loder returned to his phone booth. The one which had been occupied by Baron Crispi was once more vacant. The Baron was back in the lounge, sipping another brandy-and-vermouth.

Nita van Sloan was fiddling with her cocktail glass and consulting her watch constantly. She couldn't stand it any longer. The blood was pounding in her veins. Wentworth had been away for sixteen minutes now. She didn't know what was happening up there in Sabin's room. Dick might be dead up there. He might be in a trap and need help. She had all she could do to keep herself from running out of the lounge and taking the elevator upstairs.

And suddenly, she choked back a sob of relief. In the mirror over the bar, she saw Wentworth come into the hotel lobby from the street. His clothes were immaculate; his bearing was easy and nonchalant.

He stopped for a moment just inside the revolving doors, and scanned the occupants of the lobby. He saw Blagg come in from the side street entrance, followed by two other men, each carrying a vacuum cleaner. The two men were attired as porters.

34

They bent over the cleaners, plugging them into sockets as if they were about to start cleaning. Blagg walked steadily across the lobby, and when he passed Loder's phone booth, he nodded.

Almost at once, Baron Crispi, who had finished his drink, arose and threw down another dollar bill. "Keep the change, Thomas," he said again, as he hurried out into the street.

Wentworth was apparently unaware that he was being watched by both Loder and Blagg. He coolly lit a cigarette, and sauntered across the lobby, *but not toward the cocktail lounge.*

Out of the corner of his eye he saw Nita leaving her seat at the bar to join him, and he shook his head almost imperceptibly.

Nita saw the look in his face, and she froze where she stood. She knew her Dick like a book. She had seen that look in the past. No ordinary observer would have been able to read anything in it. But she knew that Richard Wentworth was taut and poised. She knew he was expecting attack.

She understood also, that he was making for the door instead of coming to rejoin her, because he didn't want her at his side when the attack was launched.

SWIFTLY, HER eyes swept over the lobby, seeking the possible source of danger. Her glance flicked past Blagg, past Loder, and centered on the two porters. They were apparently engaged in the very innocent occupation of hooking up two vacuum cleaners. Their bodies hid the instruments from the view of anyone in the lobby. But when they straightened up, she gasped. Although keyed up as she was to notice little things, she saw at once that there was something wrong with these two machines. The porters were straddling the long bars of the cleaners, which they were pointing in Wentworth's direction. And at the end of those long handles there was a gaping black hole exactly like the muzzle of a machine gun!

Even as Nita looked, she saw the porters flick down the switches, and in response to that motion *flame lanced from the black muzzles!* Two long, licking tongues of flame stretched forth red, blazing fingers directly at Richard Wentworth's broad back.

Nita screamed, "Dick! Behind you—"

But Wentworth must have had eyes in the back of his head. For at that exact moment—even before Nita screamed—he spun on his heel.

Two guns, one in each hand, blasted simultaneously.

The deafening thunder of those guns filled the lobby as the long, stabbing arrows of flame licked out toward him. He fired only once with each weapon. Each shot rendered one attacker helpless. They hurtled backward, dragging their flamethrowers with them. The flames were deflected from Wentworth almost as the fiery tips were about to touch him. The hot blast of those twin chutes of fire nearly seared his face. And then they were carried upward, scorching the ceiling as the nozzles were dragged backward by the collapsing porters.

The two jets of fire hissed upward, and flame began to curl around the ceiling.

The heat brought the sprinkler system into operation, and water surged downward upon the suddenly panic-stricken, shouting patrons in the lobby. Men and women began to stream for the exits, fighting and jostling one another.

Wentworth swung about lithely, knowing that the fire would

soon be extinguished by the efficient sprinkler system. He knew that Red Feather had not finished. Surely, he had other threats in reserve. Wentworth looked for more enemies. And sure enough, they came!

Men suddenly filled the main entrance, and the doorway from the side street. Others surged up from the lobby. A dozen guns were trained on him from as many directions.

Grimly, he faced the onslaught, but he held his fire, as did the men who approached him. Evidently the order was now to take him alive. More men kept streaming into the lobby from both entrances, and each man aimed a gun at Richard Wentworth.

NITA UNDERSTOOD the extreme seriousness of the situation. And what she was about to do was done instinctively—with the instinct of a woman who had learned well how to be the fighting mate of a fighting man. The vial Wentworth had given her was in her hand. As the attackers closed in, she raised it high in the air, and hurled it into the center of the lobby, directly in front of Wentworth.

The glass shattered on the floor, and immediately a white, opaque cloud of steam arose in vast, billowing folds to spread out through the lobby. It rose higher and higher, and it seemed to nurture itself, for the higher it rose the wider it spread, until it almost filled the entire room.

Wentworth dropped into a crouching position, and ran straight toward the spot where Nita had been standing. He whispered, "Nita!"

"Dick!" She murmured.

Their hands met, and then they were hurrying through the

dense white fog, feeling their way with arms outstretched. They passed into the bar, and felt their way along the wall to the street door.

Inside, Red Feather's men started shooting, angered at the realization that they had been tricked.

Out in the street, four men were standing at the curb, guns in their hands. They were the rear guard, posted in case Wentworth should break through. As they saw Nita and her tall escort leaving the hotel they immediately opened fire.

Wentworth thrust her behind him, and blasted back at them, standing spraddle-legged, so that she would not be hit. He fired each gun once, and two of the men fell wounded. And now pedestrians gathered across the street, and Wentworth dared not fire again. The remaining two, realizing their advantage, came running forward, triggering their guns. They were bent on closing up the space between them and Wentworth, so that they would be sure not to miss.

But they had not taken two steps, when a long, powerful Daimler roared up and spilled them backward as it braked to a stop directly in front of Dick and Nita. A bearded Sikh chauffeur sat at the wheel, his black, glittering eyes filled with a fierce joy.

"Shall I kill the dogs, Master?" he said in fluent Punjabi.

"Not this time, Ram Singh," Wentworth said grimly. "I want to get Miss Nita away from here. Then I must return."

He helped Nita into the car and they turned into the traffic of the avenue.

Behind them, white opaque smoke was beginning to eddy from the hotel out into the street. That was the gas from Nita's vial. It was a secret gas whose formula was known only to Wentworth and to a certain man in the War Department of the United States of America. Wentworth had developed it and had given the formula to the government, and it was being used for smoke-screens. Its swift expansive property made it ideal for such purpose. Having donated the formula anonymously, he had taken the grimly humorous opportunity to select the name by which it was referred to in the records of the War Department—*Spider Gas!*

TIMES SQUARE was shrilly alive as the white fumes of the gas came pouring out of the hotel, and fire engines clanged nearby. Police patrol cars were racing toward them from every direction, while sirens cut the air keenly. Pedestrians were keeping their distance, but watching with avid curiosity.

The Daimler was halted in a traffic jam, only a half block from the hotel. Wentworth said, "Darling, I want you to go home with Ram Singh. I must—"

Nita's eyes flashed rebelliously. "You're cutting me out of it, Dick! You promised—"

"I'm sorry, Nita. But now it's war—war between the Spider and Red Feather. And I don't want your precious safety to complicate things for me."

She sighed, realizing how right he was. "Dick," she breathed, "I'm afraid—afraid of Red Feather's mind—his devil's mind! He used fire—it was real *fire* that spouted out of those vacuum cleaners. And when that failed, Dick, he had his regular killers ready."

"I know," Wentworth said, glancing back toward the hotel. "Don't worry; I'll be on my guard every minute—"

Suddenly he stiffened, and his voice caught a whiplash of urgency: "Ram Singh! Maneuver to follow that cab! *It's part of Red Feather's underground escape system!*"

He was pointing rigidly at a taxicab which had pulled past the hotel without stopping. It had threaded its way through the frantically excited throngs of pedestrians and had swung past the Daimler on the wrong side of the street. It was now turning into a side street. The cab was almost at the end of the block, and speeding up. Upon its side was lettered the name: ONYX TAXICAB SYSTEM.

Metz had said that much—that he was to have escaped in an Onyx taxicab. Undoubtedly this cab was the one that was to have picked him up; but seeing the excitement, the driver had kept going.

Ram Singh needed no more order than that. His long experience in Wentworth's service had taught him to swing into action at the instant of command. It was that split-second timing which had more than once saved the lives of both the fighting Sikh and his fighting master. Almost before Wentworth finished talking, the Daimler was backing and weaving through traffic like a bloodhound on the scent.

"Report at home!" Wentworth flung out, and leaped to the curb.

Nita waved acknowledgment, and the car was gone.

The last glimpse Wentworth had of Nita was of her beautiful face flushed with the thrill of this new and dangerous game.

And then both the Onyx cab and the Daimler were lost to sight as they rounded the corner.

CHAPTER 4
DEATH COMES IN SIXTEEN CYLINDERS

WENTWORTH HIMSELF could not go. He must remain to explain to the police; to answer countless questions. He walked back to the hotel and at once he was surrounded by uniformed men, pressing through the entrance. The lobby was already becoming free of smoke, for the volatile Spider *Gas* was swiftly rising toward the ceiling, and disintegrating into small swirling eddies resembling midget banks of fog on a misty morning.

Something had happened to the electric light system, and the two vacuum cleaners, hooked up to the hotel current, had ceased to spurt flame. The fire was already out, due to the swift operation of the sprinkler outlets.

When the police surged into the lobby, they found it in utter darkness. Their flashlights etched out the forms of the two wounded porters, now conscious. Otherwise, the place was deserted. Red Feather's killers had fled.

Wentworth found himself besieged by questioners, from a local precinct captain up to an Inspector of Homicide. He explained very sparingly, saying only that he had been suddenly attacked by the flamethrowers, and had defended himself. As to the reasons for the attack, he only shrugged his shoulders.

41

"Perhaps they mistook me for someone else," he said.

"For instance," a voice broke in ironically behind him, *"for the Spider?"*

Wentworth whirled, as the captain and the inspector stiffened, and saluted respectfully.

The new arrival was a ruddy complexioned, stockily built man, who carried himself with an air of quiet but efficient authority. Stanley Kirkpatrick, Commissioner of Police of the City of New York, was without question the outstanding police executive in the country. Beloved by the entire force, he also enjoyed the complete respect and confidence of the civilian public.

For many years now, Kirkpatrick had waged relentless war against the Spider, while being at the same time a close friend of Richard Wentworth. Commissioner Kirkpatrick was a sworn servant of the Law and hated with all his soul the unorthodox methods which the Spider employed against the underworld. And in spite of the warm friendship between the two men, Wentworth understood clearly that if ever the Commissioner should obtain definite proof that Richard Wentworth was the Spider—then their friendship would be superseded by Kirkpatrick's devotion to the Law.

Many times in the past, the Commissioner had had reason to believe that his friend was really the Spider. But Wentworth had cleverly managed to nullify that suspicion.

Now however, it was coming once more to the fore.

Kirkpatrick gazed bleakly around the lobby, eyeing the

wounded men. The police were already questioning them, while they were being treated by police surgeons. But they maintained a stubborn silence, refusing to answer all questions.

THE COMMISSIONER swore softly under his breath. "They're like all the other agents of Red Feather. They won't talk. One would think they were more afraid of Red Feather than of the electric chair!"

"There are worse things than the electric chair!" Wentworth said softly.

Kirkpatrick swung on him, gray eyes glinting shrewdly. "It was you they were after, wasn't it, Dick?"

"Yes," said Wentworth. "They were after me."

"*Why?*" rapped Kirkpatrick.

"I haven't the faintest notion, Kirk."

"Do you mean those men attacked you without provocation?"

"Yes."

"That's ridiculous on the face of it, Dick, and you know it. I demand to know why they attacked you!"

"Permit me to suggest, Kirk, that you ask these men. They are the proper ones to answer such a question. Since when have the police begun to give the third degree to the *victims* of crime?"

Kirkpatrick scowled. "Damn it, Dick—"

He broke off as a uniformed patrolman entered the lobby and approached him. "Pardon, sir. There's a lady outside asking to see Mr. Wentworth. A Mrs. Blount, she says. She claims Mr. Wentworth knows her."

"Of course," said Dick. "Will you pardon me, Kirk?"

"I'll go out with you," the Commissioner grumbled. "I'm not

through asking you questions. And I don't want you walking away on me."

Wentworth shrugged, and led the way outside. The police were keeping a cleared space in front of the hotel, and the crowd of curiosity seekers was pressing in for a closer view of the wounded as they were carried to the ambulance.

A few feet away from the curb, a sixteen-cylinder car was idling. A woman of about forty was at the wheel. She was beau-

tiful in a stately, aristocratic sort of way, and she was attired in the most becoming clothes money could buy. Mrs. Irene Blount, widow of the airplane manufacturer, Norton Blount, moved only in exclusive social circles.

Only two weeks ago she had spent twenty thousand dollars for the debut of her daughter, Ellen, whom she idolized. Wentworth had met both mother and daughter in many of the homes of the Long Island social set, but he couldn't imagine why Mrs.

Blount should be driving her own car here—or why she should come expressly to see him.

He let Kirkpatrick wait at the curb and stepped out alongside the limousine.

"How do you do, Mrs. Blount? Is there anything I can do for you? How is Ellen?"

Irene Blount seemed to be under some sort of terrific nervous tension. Her hands were in her lap, but her breasts were rising and falling swiftly, and the color that suffused her cheeks was almost hectic. She looked at Wentworth queerly.

"God forgive me, Mr. Wentworth, I have come here to do a terrible thing!" She shuddered. "What am I saying! Never in this life, or the next, will I earn forgiveness for—for what I am about to do now!"

Wentworth frowned. "Surely you can't be as wicked as that, Mrs. Blount. What is it that you're going to do?"

"*This!*" she cried. Her hand came up from her lap, gripping a small twenty-two caliber pistol.

"*Richard Wentworth, I'm going to kill you!*"

The look in her face was a terrible one. To Wentworth it seemed that all the instincts of refinement and culture and humanity with which he knew her to be endowed, were being consumed within her breast by a raging inferno of pain and agony—a pain and agony not of the body, but of her very soul.

He knew in a single instant that Mrs. Blount was doing this at the order of Red Feather. Somehow, Red Feather had means of compelling this beautiful aristocrat to do a thing which shattered the very fiber of her soul.

HER HAND was clamped around the butt of the pistol, and her finger was taut upon the trigger. The horrible agony in her eyes leaped across the small intervening space between herself and Wentworth with a look that seemed to beg forgiveness and understanding, even as she killed him.

Someone shouted hoarsely behind him, and Wentworth knew it was Kirkpatrick, who had been watching the whole procedure.

But there was nothing the Commissioner could do to save him. There was only one thing Wentworth could do to save himself. He'd had ample warning as Irene Blount brought the gun up over the window ledge of the limousine. More than once had he faced drawn guns in the hands of dangerous men; and more than once had the legerdemain of his swiftly moving hands beaten those gunmen to the kill. Men with guns in their hands, facing an apparently unarmed Spider, had died with faces frozen into stupefaction, not knowing even in death whence had come the blasting automatics which had suddenly appeared in the grip of that sinister, cloaked figure.

So, Richard Wentworth could easily have drawn and fired before Irene Blount brought her gun into position. But the only part of her that was exposed to a bullet was her face and throat, and the lovely curve of her breast. Anywhere he hit her with the powerful driving force of his heavy automatics, would mean death for this woman. And knowing that she was doing this hideous thing because of some terrible compulsion, he could no more have brought himself to kill her than to kill a newborn baby.

The startled shout of Commissioner Kirkpatrick was still ringing in his ears as Irene Blount pointed the gun at his heart.

And he did not move.

Perhaps if he had leaped toward her in an effort to deflect the gun, or if he had attempted to turn and run, she might have pulled the trigger. But as she saw him standing there, cool and collected, perhaps the sight of his manifest courage did something that nothing else could have accomplished. Perhaps it lit within her once more the torch of decency which was her birthright, and which must have been smothered under the terrible compulsion which was driving her to this crime.

She stared at him, with her finger taut against the trigger. And she did not shoot. Instead, a strange and hungry light came into her eyes, as if she were seeing a new and unimagined thing which might yet be her salvation.

"Don't—aren't you—afraid to die?" she faltered.

Wentworth smiled. "There are many things that are worse than death," he said gently.

All of the sudden, a great trembling seized her body. A choked cry of misery escaped from her throat.

"Yes, yes!" she gasped. "Much worse than death!"

Suddenly, a great light of resolve came into her eyes.

"Richard Wentworth," she said in a voice grown strong and resolute, "you have shown me the way out. Thank God!"

And without warning she turned the pistol upon her breast and pulled the trigger!

Wentworth had no chance to stop her. The bullet plowed

through the white, quivering flesh just above the heart. She jerked spasmodically, and slumped over the wheel.

CHAPTER 5
"FOLLOW RICHARD
WENTWORTH!"

"**B**Y THE Lord Harry!" Commissioner Kirkpatrick exploded. "I'll have a straight answer out of you, Dick Wentworth, if I have to choke it out of you!"

Wentworth shrugged. "I'm sorry, Kirk. I've told you everything I can."

It was almost an hour after Irene Blount's dramatic suicide. Kirkpatrick and Wentworth were in the office of the manager of the Mallard Hotel. Scores of detectives were still investigating throughout the great hostelry, piecing together the actions of Red Feather's agents previous to the moment they had unleashed the flamethrowers upon Wentworth.

And Kirkpatrick was still doggedly at it.

"Dick," he said tightly, "I want to know why Irene Blount tried to shoot you, and then turned the gun upon herself."

"I've told you every word we both said." Wentworth sighed wearily. "I've repeated the story a dozen times. There's nothing more."

"All right, then. Let's get to something else. What were you doing in the hotel?"

"I was just having a Martini with Nita."

"You had no other purpose in coming here?"

"What other purpose would I have?"

"Maybe you were trying to get Red Feather?"

Abruptly, Wentworth arose. "I'm sorry, Kirk. I can't submit to this quizzing any longer. I have many things to do. With your permission, I'll be leaving—unless you want to arrest me formally."

The Commissioner sighed, and stood up. "Look here, Dick," he said. "Why won't you cooperate with me? I need all the help I can get. Red Feather has some terrible power over men and women, a power that forces them to commit stupendous crimes. Metz didn't need the money he stole. Irene Blount surely had no motive for attempting to kill you. Yet they both were driven by an evil genius they couldn't resist. Laura Burgess tried to defy him—and she died horribly under the fire of a flamethrower."

"I know all that, Kirk," Wentworth said harshly. "And believe me; I shall help you all I can."

Kirkpatrick shook his head. "Let's talk plainly for once, Dick. The Spider came here tonight to fight Red Feather in the Spider's usual way. Wouldn't it have been better if the Spider had turned over his information to the police?"

"No," said Wentworth.

"Damn it, Dick, *why not?*"

Wentworth stared at him uncompromisingly. "If I were the Spider, Kirk—as you insinuate—I would do just what the Spider did tonight. I would go after Red Feather with the same kind of weapons Red Feather uses, swift and merciless death." As he continued his voice became hard, fraught with subdued passion. "You—the police—are hampered. Your hands are tied because you must produce evidence that will stand up in court. And Red Feather is too clever ever to allow you to obtain such evidence. But the Spider is not hampered. If the Spider finds Red Feather, then Red Feather will not live to beat the case!"

Kirkpatrick's scowl became deeper as Wentworth concluded. "All right, Dick, if that's the way you look at it—I wash my hands. You and I don't see eye to eye. If you persist—"

"Wait!" Wentworth raised a hand. "You're assuming that *I* am the Spider?"

THE COMMISSIONER waved a hand impatiently. "Let's do away with pretense, Dick, for this once. Yes, I'm sure you're the Spider. And if I had evidence, I'd arrest you and see that you were convicted. I'm sworn to uphold the Law, and by God I'll uphold it, even if it means the end of our friendship!"

Wentworth nodded brusquely. "So be it, Kirk!"

He turned toward the door, moving very slowly. He put his hand on the knob, but before turning it, he looked back. Kirkpatrick was watching him, and there was the shadow of pain in the Commissioner's eyes.

A slow smile illuminated Wentworth's features. He extended his hand. "Let's shake—just this once more, Kirk!"

Kirkpatrick choked back a tightness in his throat as he accepted the proffered hand.

Silently, the two men stood there.

Then, without saying another word, Richard Wentworth turned and went out of the room. He walked through the lobby with a set and expressionless face.

Commissioner Kirkpatrick came out after him. His lips were

tight, and he was holding himself rigid. His eyes followed Wentworth's broad back to the revolving doors.

"Murdoch!" he snapped to one of the detectives in the lobby. "Follow that man! Take as many plainclothes officers as you need. *I want Richard Wentworth shadowed every minute of the day and night!*"

CHAPTER 6
THE NUMBERS GAME

A S RICHARD WENTWORTH strode away, he did not look to the right or left.

Murdoch had signaled to two other plainclothesmen, and whispered to them swiftly. One of the detectives remained with him and followed Wentworth on foot, while the third got into a police squad car and crawled along behind them. In this way, none of the trailers would be left flatfooted by any sudden moves of the quarry.

None of the detectives noted, however, that there were still others who were interested in the movements of Richard Wentworth. They did not see the flat-nosed man or the man in the black fedora that moved inconspicuously through the crowds in his wake.

Loder kept about twenty feet behind the detectives, and Blagg hailed a taxicab.

"Follow that man in the black fedora," he ordered, indicating Loder.

Thus, Wentworth seemed to be the unconscious head of a

shadow parade up Broadway. None of his actions indicated that he was in any way cognizant of these attentions. He walked swiftly and purposefully to the corner, and swung west. He entered a cigar store in the middle of the block and dialed the number of his penthouse apartment on East End Avenue. Since the destruction of his previous great, fortress-like retreat, he had decided to make his headquarters in no one certain place, where he would be the focus of attack for any enemy who guessed his association with the Spider.

In conformity with his policy, he now had four apartments in various parts of the city, in addition to four or five furnished rooms and hotel rooms in easily accessible spots. Thus, he was never far from sanctuary if he should be hard-pressed. But he had worked out a code with Ram Singh and Nita, so that when he said: *"Report at home!"* they had known by the word *home* that he meant the East End Avenue Apartment. Had he said, *"At the apartment,"* it would have designated a private house in Greenwich Village, which he had leased for ten years. He had various designations for each location, which had been committed to memory.

HE NOW waited while the dial tone buzzed six times. He clicked the hook down on the sixth note, waited a moment, and then lifted it again. The interruption had not been long enough to kill the connection entirely, so that the dial tone was immediately resumed. He let it buzz six times more, disconnected for another moment, and then allowed it to ring on. That was his identification signal. Ram Singh would know it was he who was calling. In this way, it would not be necessary to answer any calls except those from Wentworth.

Now however, as he held the receiver to his ear, a sudden foreboding of evil swept over him. There was no answer to his call.

There had been plenty of time for Ram Singh and Nita to tail the Onyx cab and return to the East End Avenue address.

Wentworth held the receiver to his ear for a full minute, while he turned in such a way as to look out of the phone booth without seeming to do so. His eyes glinted as he noted a police squad car cruising slowly past the store, and a detective standing directly across the street. Wentworth's camera eye had recorded the face of that detective as having been among those in the Mallard Hotel lobby. It was clear to him that Kirkpatrick intended to keep close tabs upon him.

This did not bother him as much as the silence from the East End Apartment. He started to hang up, when he suddenly noticed something else that brought a frown to his face. A man strolling past the cigar store stopped just outside the window and casually lit a cigarette. That man, too, Wentworth recognized, though he had caught only a flashing glimpse of him in the Hotel Mallard lobby just before he was attacked.

It was the flat-nosed Blagg.

HE DID not know the man's name, of course, nor did he know that Blagg had attempted to follow him from the cocktail lounge, and had been outmaneuvered by Nita. There had been no time for her to tell him about that in the Daimler. But he did know two things: First, that the flat-nosed man had been in the Mallard lobby; second, that he was here now. They added up to a single conclusion—the flat-nosed man was an agent of Red Feather.

Wentworth's decision was quickly made. He hung up and stepped purposefully from the store. He did not look at Blagg directly, but out of the corner of his eye he saw the man signal to someone in a taxicab which was parked farther down the street. Blagg had changed places with Loder, so that the quarry would not notice that he was being followed by any particular man.

Wentworth continued down the block, apparently oblivious of any trailers. He turned the corner and went north on Eighth Avenue until he arrived at the West View Hotel, a small, cheap hostelry which catered to transients, but which rented a few rooms on a permanent basis. Boldly, he entered the lobby and stepped up to the desk.

"I want a room for tonight," he said.

"Any baggage?" the clerk asked.

"No."

"That'll be two-fifty, sir, in advance."

Wentworth paid, and signed the register. Since he had no luggage, the clerk gave him the key, dispensing with a bell boy, and Wentworth took the elevator up to the sixth floor. His room was 612.

The operator said, "Six-twelve is to your right—the end of the hall, right near the stairs."

"Thanks," Wentworth said, and started down the corridor.

He knew very well where room 612 was located. In fact he had asked the clerk to give him a room with western exposure, because he wanted one near the stairs.

He inserted the key in the lock, and pushed the door open. The operator waited only to see that he found his room, and then he shut the gate and sent the cage down.

Immediately, Wentworth took the key out of the lock, without even opening the door. Two strides brought him to the stairway, and he raced down to the fifth floor. He stopped before the door of Room 514 and brought out a small, compact key container. Each key had a numbered tag which was treated with phosphorus so that it would show up in the dark. He selected key number eight and inserted it in the lock. In a moment he was inside. As he closed the door, he noticed the elevator indicator advance upward and stop at six. He smiled grimly. His pursuers were already bottling him up. A police detective or one of Red Feather's men had also taken a room on the sixth floor. There would be others covering the hotel exits, in case he should slip past the watchful gaze of the sixth floor sentries.

Once inside, he set quickly to work. Before he was halfway across the room, he had stripped off his overcoat, jacket and vest. He removed his tie, shirt and trousers, and seated himself before the dresser, clad only in his underwear.

From the top drawer of the dresser he took a black lacquered box which opened only when he pressed two sides simultaneously in certain places. The cover slid open, revealing a complete makeup kit, together with a spare automatic and two extra clips.

This was one of the rooms Wentworth maintained under a

completely different identity. The clerk downstairs knew only that the tenant of 514 was one Joseph Moulton. He knew vaguely that Moulton was connected with one of the large Manhattan gambling syndicates, and that he traveled extensively, handling large bets. Therefore, his room might be unused for weeks at a time. But the rent was always paid three months in advance, so no one in the hotel ever worried about Joe Moulton's actions.

SEATED BEFORE the mirror, Wentworth's swift fingers worked surely and skillfully upon his countenance, employing materials from the makeup box. In a small frame on the dresser he had a photograph of himself made up as Joe Moulton, and he used this picture as a guide.

A little plastic material transformed his face from the lean hard features of Richard Wentworth to the somewhat puffy face of Joe Moulton. A touch of shadow dye under the eyes gave the effect of deep hollows, indicative of dissipation. Paper-thin aluminum plates inserted in the nostrils broadened the nose; and false tooth bridges changed Wentworth's own perfectly white and even teeth into a mouthful of crooked bicuspids and molars liberally furnished with gold caps. A wig of dun colored hair completed the change, and Richard Wentworth gazed with satisfaction into the mirror which revealed the personality of Joe Moulton, gambler.

Satisfied that he had omitted no detail which might betray him, he locked the make-up box and put it away. From a trunk in the closet he took a new tan suit, a tan shirt with tie to match, tan shoes and overcoat. He put these on, and inserted in his tie a huge two carat diamond stickpin. He carefully packed the discarded clothes away, once more locking the trunk.

As he paced up and down the room two or three times, it was amazing to see how the characteristic mannerisms and walk of Richard Wentworth had disappeared to give way to those of Joe Moulton. The only garment Wentworth retained of his old belongings was a thin rubber cape with a purple back, of such fine texture that it could be rolled to fit in his back pocket. And there was a black slouch hat of the same material, together with a small, flat makeup case—only such essentials as would be necessary to use should he suddenly have occasion to appear as the Spider.

With a last glance about the room to make sure that he had left nothing incriminating in view, he snapped the switch lights and went out.

WHEN THE cage stopped at the floor in answer to his ring, the operator said, "Hello, Mr. Moulton. I didn't know you were in. You been away?"

"Yeah," Wentworth said in a nasal voice. "I been in Chi. Got in this morning. Guess you were off. Anything new around this dump?"

"Nothing much, Mr. Moulton. Except some guy just checked in on the sixth floor, and it looks like the cops is after him. One of the cops took a room on the same floor, and there's another one parked in the lobby. And just now another bozo takes a room on the sixth floor, and slips me a sawbuck not to mention it to the cop downstairs."

"Is that so?" Wentworth said. "What rooms did these three

guys take? Maybe if we combine the numbers, we can hit a winner in the numbers."

"Say, that's an idea!" the operator exclaimed. "This guy Wentworth has six-twelve. The cop took six-fourteen, next door, and the other guy—he's registered under the name of Max Loder—took six-eleven, right across the hall."

"Six-eleven, six-twelve and six-fourteen, huh," Wentworth repeated. "Lemme think about them. When I come back I'll tell you if I figured a good combination."

As he got out of the cage, he saw Detective Murdoch seated near the front door, reading a newspaper. Blagg, the flat-nosed man, was at the cigar counter, kibitzing with the sales girl. Both Murdoch and Blagg gave Wentworth the once-over, and immediately lost interest in him.

Wentworth smiled grimly. He had been sure his disguise would pass muster. He waved to the night clerk, and crossed the lobby to the small office at the rear where the switchboard was located.

"Hello, Mamie," he said to the operator.

"Why, hello, Mr. Moulton!" she said. "Gee, I haven't seen you for a month. I never got a chance to thank you for the ten dollars you left me for Christmas."

"That's all right, Mamie," Wentworth said, making sure that the door of the switchboard room was closed so that neither Murdoch nor Blagg could see what was going on. He leaned over the board and lowered his voice.

"Would you like to make twenty bucks?"

"You don't have to ask, Mr. Moulton!"

"Okay. There's a guy in six-eleven who's got some inside dope on the horses at Tropical Park. If he should make any calls…."

"Sure," Mamie said. "I get you."

He slipped two ten dollar bills over the top of the board.

"Just wait in the lobby," Mamie told him. "If six-eleven gets any calls, or makes any, I'll hold up the connection and page you. You take the desk phone, and I'll leave the board open so you can hear the conversation."

"Right," said Wentworth.

He returned to the lobby and entered the public phone booth. Once more he dialed the East End Avenue apartment, and once more he got a no answer signal. His lips tightened.

He went over to the cigar counter and bought a package of chewing gum and a copy of *Ace G-Man Magazine.* Then he sat down in a chair next to Detective Murdoch.

"Kinda cold today, ain't it?" he said in his newly assumed nasal voice.

Murdoch grunted, but did not reply.

Blagg had left the cigar counter and was now playing a pinball game at the other side of the lobby.

It was a tribute to Richard Wentworth's self-control that he could sit and read a magazine with such an attitude of cool unconcern, when he knew that Nita and Ram Singh must have fallen into some position of unknown danger as a result of following the Onyx cab. Otherwise, one of them would surely have managed to return to the East End Avenue address to report when he called.

And he, Wentworth, could do nothing but sit here and wait....

IT WAS only ten minutes, but it seemed an hour, before the phone on the desk rang, and the clerk answered it, and then called out:

"Mr. Moulton—phone call!"

Wentworth arose and hurried over to the desk. He knew that the eyes of both Murdoch and Blagg were on him, if for no other reason than curiosity. But he knew that their curiosity would swiftly be turned to suspicion if they saw him merely holding the receiver without speaking. On the other hand, he could not speak into the phone without warning the man in 611 that someone was listening to his conversation.

Wentworth had foreseen this difficulty, and prepared for it. He had surreptitiously torn a piece off the back cover of his magazine, and had folded it in several thicknesses to fit into the telephone mouthpiece. And as he picked up the receiver, his right hand slipped up over the phone and stuffed the heavy folded paper into the cup. He pressed it far in against the diaphragm. Now, he could speak into it and his voice would merely rebound from the paper without being transmitted through the open line.

He had the receiver at his ear, and caught the following conversation:

"Thirteen."

"Seven."

"Twenty-six. Loder speaking. I have that man under observation. He's across the hall from me."

To give the appearance of carrying on a conversation, Wentworth spoke into the transmitter, repeating the words that were being said over the line. In this way he was also better able to memorize them. The cold voice at the other end was speaking.

"How do you know he can't get out some other way than through the hall?"

"He can't. It's a sixth floor window facing on the street. Blagg is in the lobby. He's paying a newsboy to watch that window. I'm sure our man is safe."

"Very well. We will make certain that nothing slips up this time. I am sending Kranz and four men to assist you. It is highly important that the person we are speaking of be liquidated at once. As soon as you have finished there, you will proceed immediately to take charge of the covering force at the Mandalay operation. That is all!"

The cold voice stopped and Wentworth heard the disconnecting click. As he hung up, his eyes were filled with swift speculation. He had learned two things: First, that killers were coming here at once; second, that Red Feather was planning another crime—*the Mandalay Operation*. Those three words puzzled him. Red Feather couldn't, of course, have referred to the city of Mandalay....

Wentworth pushed that puzzle to the back of his mind under the pressure of the more immediate danger. Those killers coming here must be stopped, and stopped swiftly before they made a shambles of this place, as they had done of the Mallard. He hurried across to the public phone booth. If he could reach Commissioner Kirkpatrick, it might be possible to get police reserves on the spot.

HE WAS halfway across the lobby when he suddenly broke his stride, his lips narrowing into a thin, tight line.

Through the glass door of the hotel he saw a small truck pulling up squarely in front of the entrance. The driver remained at the wheel, but five men emerged from the tonneau and advanced to the hotel in a close-knit, compact group. Three of them were carrying bulky objects, loosely covered by oilskin sheets.

In a flash, Wentworth realized that he had underestimated Red Feather.

Red Feather had taken into account the fact that someone might overhear that conversation with Loder. Therefore, he had dispatched these killers, *before* calling, thereby timing their arrival in order to preclude any leeway of warning the police.

Wentworth turned on his heel. Instead of making for the phone booth, he headed swiftly for the men's room at the rear of the lobby. The first of that compact group of killers was coming through the revolving doors as Wentworth disappeared.

One by one they entered. Their leader, a stocky, bullet-headed man in a tight-fitting Chesterfield and black derby, was carrying one of the oilskin-covered objects. He crossed to the clerk's desk and said, "Take it easy, punk!"

The others advanced into the lobby spreading out as they came in, and throwing the oilskin covers off their packages, to reveal shiny machine-guns!

The leader, Kranz, looked over toward Blagg, who had stopped playing the pinball game. Blagg nodded almost imperceptibly toward Detective Murdoch, who was coming out of his chair and clawing at his gun. Blagg did not wait. He hurried out past the gunmen, and disappeared into the street.

Kranz grinned and raised the machine gun, covering Murdoch. "Hold it, copper!" he grated.

The other men headed for the elevator, and one of them pushed the button violently to summon the cage.

Murdoch was no coward. He kept going for his gun.

Kranz's lips curled. "Okay, copper. Take it!"

His finger was on the trip, when suddenly, from the rear of the lobby near the men's room, came the queer, bloodcurdling sound of laughter!

Every eye in the lobby was turned toward that sound. With guns suspended in midair, those men looked to see who was laughing at such a time.

And they beheld a grim, cloaked figure whose hideous face was almost covered by a black slouch hat. From under the cape, two hands were thrust. And each hand held a heavy black automatic!

"*The Spider!*" shouted one of the killers.

And then all hell broke loose in that lobby.

CHAPTER 7
JOE MOULTON KEEPS AN
APPOINTMENT

T HE GREATEST soldier of all time, Napoleon Bonaparte, owed most of his military successes to the element of surprise. Time and again he defeated vastly superior enemies by striking unexpectedly. He generally attacked one flank of the opposing army, the strongest, and destroyed it, thus rendering the enemy impotent.

Thus did the Spider fight tonight.

The odds were one against five. But the Spider had two powerful allies—surprise and accuracy.

Those two automatics, peeping out from under the black cloak, thundered into action in a thrilling melody of rhythmic doom as they blasted their messages of death into the bodies of Red Feather's paid killers. Their machine-guns, lumbering into action, sprayed lead all around the dreadful cloaked figure which stood there, fearless and scornful of cover.

Detective Murdoch was forgotten as these gunmen swung their weapons to blast at the Spider. Flame and lead belched from the muzzles. But even as they rattled their staccato patter, their bursts went wild, stabbing zigzag lines of steel jacketed bullets into the walls on all sides—for the machine-guns were held by dead hands.

The Spider's twin automatics had turned first upon those men who held the Thompsons, for they were the most dangerous. The two by the elevator door were dropped by the Spider's first two shots and Kranz by the third. All three of them had pulled the trips of their guns, but they had fired too quickly, before lining the sights upon the black cloaked enemy. They never fired a second burst, because they were dead before the thunder of their first shots ceased to echo back from the ceiling.

And the two remaining killers, who were armed only with revolvers, turned and ran for dear life, heading wildly and frantically back toward the street door where their truck was waiting.

But now, Detective Murdoch had his gun out of its holster, and he covered the fleeing gunmen, shouting to them to halt. The killers turned to snap shots at him, and Murdoch fired twice, swiftly, hitting both men at close range.

Then, with eyes glittering, the detective swung toward the rear of the lobby, bringing his smoking service revolver around.

"You, too, Spider—"

He stopped, with mouth agape, for he was talking to thin air.

The Spider's twin automatics were turned upon the machine gunners.

The Spider had disappeared!

Neither the hotel clerk nor the girl at the cigar counter was in sight. They had both taken refuge by dropping to the floor, and there they remained, shivering with fright.

Detective Murdoch uttered an angry oath and sprang across the lobby, jumping over the bodies of Kranz and the other dead machine gunners. He wrenched open the door of the men's room, and stared grimly at the window opposite—a window wide open in mute testimony as to the Spider's path of escape. ON THE floor near the washbasin, the puffy faced Joe Moulton was staggering to his feet, one hand at his head. He wobbled a bit and muttered hoarsely, "The Spider—knocked me out!"

Detective Murdoch swore harshly, and leaped across the room to the window. He threw a leg over, and jumped out into the alley in wild pursuit of his quarry. But the representative of law and order was greatly disappointed to find, when he came out on the street, that the Spider had vanished.

Back in the washroom, Joe Moulton seemed to revive from his state of apparent collapse the moment Detective Murdoch climbed out of the window.

In fact, his revival was so swift that it would have seemed suspicious to anyone watching him.

He was, however, unobserved as he slipped out of the washroom and hurried through the lobby. Somewhere in the distance, a police car siren was shrieking. The lobby was deserted except for the dead bodies of Kranz and the other gunmen. The desk clerk and the cigar counter girl were both keeping out of sight.

Joe Moulton did not at once depart. He stopped in the lobby

and did a peculiar thing. From his pocket he drew a chromium cigar lighter. A flip of his finger opened it at the bottom, and with this instrument in his hand he hastened from one body to another, pressing the bottom of the lighter to the forehead of each of the dead gunmen who had died under the Spider's guns. Only when he had finished that task did Moulton straighten up and walk out through the front door. Behind him, on the floor of the lobby, the stark dead men now bore peculiar marks on their foreheads. On each one was a glowing red reproduction of a spider.

The dead men lay there for all to see—and to know they had died by the hand of the Spider.

Moulton mingled with the excited crowd that was thronging close to the hotel entrance to see what had happened. Questions were flung at him, and he answered them all by saying that there had been a shooting inside.

"Better not stick around!" he shouted. "I think the killers are coming back!"

In the confusion, he made his way down the street, and was gone before the first police car arrived.

There was no satisfaction in his eyes as he hurried away. For, although he had succeeded in thwarting the agents of Red Feather in this instance, he knew very well that he had not crippled the vicious organization of which that sinister person was the head. Somewhere in the city another stupendous crime was in preparation—one which even now might be progressing to a bloody climax. The words he had overheard on the phone were etched in his mind—*the Mandalay Operation!* If he could only guess what that phrase referred to, he would know where Red Feather was going to strike next!

WENTWORTH'S RUSE in assuming the character of Joe Moulton had not been entirely for the purpose of evading his shadowers. Under the name of Moulton he had established many connections in the sporting world. Joe Moulton was known as a man who could handle a bet of any size, and who could be trusted with the details of confidential transactions. Thus, he was often called upon as a go-between when delicate negotiations were in progress. None of the people with whom he dealt knew the origin of the substantial funds which seemed to be always at his command.

And it was this financial stability which supported the fiction of the huge syndicate supposedly backing him. In all transactions he was careful to keep his own name in the background as far as the public was concerned. He sought no publicity. It was not strange, therefore, that neither the public nor the newspapers were aware of the fact that Joe Moulton had been largely instrumental in arranging the last three heavyweight matches, as well as a number of other sporting events which might otherwise have been unsuccessful.

So he had not been unduly surprised when he received word that morning that Carl Webster, the horse-racing magnate, wanted to see him. All calls for Joe Moulton came to the West View Hotel, and were then relayed by Mamie to a certain address which he had given her, supposedly that of a brother. When he received the message he had at once phoned Carl Webster.

"I've got to see you tonight without fail, Joe!" Webster had said thickly. "It—it's damned important!"

"I may be busy tonight, Mr. Webster. How about tomorrow morning?"

"No, no, Joe. For God's sake, don't fail me. Cancel any other plans you may have for tonight. Come to see me at eleven o'clock. It—it's a matter of life and death, Joe!"

"Life and death? What do you mean, Mr. Webster?"

Webster's voice had dropped almost to a whisper. "You've heard of—*Red Feather?*"

Wentworth's pulse had begun to race.

"What about Red Feather?"

"I can't tell you any more over the phone, Joe. But you've got to come at eleven o'clock tonight. Promise!"

"All right," Wentworth had promised.

And now, in spite of the fact that he was worried about Nita and Ram Singh, he must keep his word and go to see Carl Webster.

Webster's office was only a few blocks north, opposite Madison Square Garden. As Wentworth walked swiftly in that direction, police radio cars whizzed past, going south toward the West View Hotel. He smiled grimly. Twice tonight he had balked the undertakings of Red Feather's hirelings, with serious loss to them. But he knew well that Red Feather must have many such men at his command. And there was still the puzzle of the *Mandalay Operation*. Whether his visit to Carl Webster would yield any concrete clue to the identity of Red Feather, he could not tell. But he must follow up every slightest possibil-

71

ity—for he realized that in this war between himself and Red Feather, he—Wentworth—was at a distinct disadvantage, for Red Feather had guessed the identity of the Spider.

From now on, all the resources of this brilliant criminal's vicious organization would be devoted to the destruction of Richard Wentworth. For himself, Wentworth did not mind such attention. In fact, he would have welcomed further attempts against himself, for each attempt gave him renewed opportunity to seek contact with Red Feather. It was for Nita, however, that he experienced anxiety. Knowing that Wentworth was the Spider, what better means could Red Feather find for striking against him than through Nita van Sloan?

A BLOCK from Carl Webster's office, Wentworth entered a drug store and once more phoned the East End Avenue apartment. Still there was no answer. Now, his premonition was reduced almost to a certainty. Somehow, Nita and Ram Singh had met with disaster!

Impatiently, he hurried toward the Webster Building. It was five minutes to eleven by his wrist watch, and he hoped to finish quickly whatever business Carl Webster had in mind, so that he would lose no time in locating Nita.

As he approached the entrance of the building, he saw little Tommy Tildon, the newsboy who always sold the sporting extras in front of Madison Square Garden as the crowds came out. Tommy's left leg was a half inch shorter than his right, as a result of a hit-and-run accident six years ago. Everybody bought papers from him, because they knew he was saving money to have an operation. Wentworth had several times offered to advance the money, but Tommy wouldn't take it, insisting that he must be able to see his way clear to repaying it before he could accept such a loan. Wentworth admired the boy's guts, and he had found a good job for Tommy's pretty, older sister, Lillian, as secretary to Carl Webster.

Ordinarily, Tommy's thin, almost elfin face, would be bright and smiling, in spite of the constant pain of his left leg. And his cheerful voice could be heard above the rumble of traffic, calling out the latest extra. But tonight, as Wentworth neared him, he saw that the boy's face was set and unsmiling.

Tommy was standing close to the curb, watching the traffic swirl past. He was not crying out his wares. His papers were bundled under his left arm, and his right hand was fumbling with something hidden under the threadbare coat.

Richard Wentworth was still perhaps thirty feet away when he saw what Tommy Tildon was watching. A black town car with license plates numbered W-2 was swinging to the curb. That would be Carl Webster's car. The racing magnate was just arriving in time for his appointment with Joe Moulton. Wentworth recognized Mike Stockly, Webster's chauffeur, as he climbed out from behind the wheel to hold the door open for his employer.

And then, things began to happen with gruesome swiftness. CARL WEBSTER was stepping out of the town car; one foot was on the running board, and the other on the sidewalk. Less than six feet away from him, little Tommy Tildon suddenly let the newspapers drop to the ground. From beneath his coat he brought a small automatic pistol and pointed it at the racing magnate.

For an instant, Carl Webster thought it was some sort of boyish prank. His kindly eyes twinkled.

"What is it, Tommy?" he asked, smiling. "A new kind of water pistol?"

Tommy didn't answer. His hand shook as he kept the gun pointed; his finger curled around the trigger. Even though he was unsteady, he couldn't miss at that distance.

Too late, Carl Webster realized that it was not a water pistol Tommy was holding, nor was he playing a childish prank. His face tightened into cold, fatalistic lines.

"I know why you're doing it, Tommy," he whispered. "May God forgive you—"

Mike Stockly, the chauffeur, had not even been looking at the little newsboy. But, at his master's words, he swung around, staring at the frail lad with the gun.

Tommy's finger was beginning to contract on the trigger. His thin face was taut with emotion, and real hatred flared in his eyes—hatred which was inexplicable because Webster had always been more than kind to Tommy and his sister.

"Damn you! Damn you!" he screamed. And he pressed the trigger.

No one was close enough to stop the boy. No one was close enough to save Carl Webster from the death which would spit from the black muzzle of that pistol. Not even Richard Wentworth, who was still almost fifteen feet away!

Wentworth saw the whole thing as if it were a scene from

a motion picture being filmed in the street. When the papers dropped from Tommy's hand, and the gun came out, Wentworth knew that this was no prank. Trained as he was to judge human beings by their attitude, to read a man's intentions from little movements like the hunching of a shoulder or the clenching of a hand, he knew with sure instinct that Tommy Tildon intended to kill Carl Webster.

The average man would have been so astounded by the realization of the boy's intention as to be frozen into immobility—as Mike Stockly had been. Not, however, Richard Wentworth. His uncannily accurate ability for measuring space and time in an emergency, to the hair's breadth of an inch, told him that he could not reach Tommy before the boy would shoot.

But beside him on the sidewalk there was a tall, wire meshed trash basket, such as the city provides for rubbish. Wentworth seized this basket and whirled it with a swift, powerful motion which sent the refuse can skidding along the sidewalk to smash against Tommy Tildon's back at the very instant he pulled the trigger.

Tommy was thrown forward by the impact of the basket. He went stumbling toward the town car, and the gun in his hand exploded harmlessly, as the slug thudded into the running board.

The boy caught his balance and twisted around, raising the gun once more, grimly resolved to kill this man. But now Wentworth had reached him. He struck down with the edge of his hand upon Tommy's wrist, knocking the gun from the lad's hand. The weapon struck the running board, and Wentworth swooped and snatched it up.

MIKE STOCKLY now sprang forward, aiming a terrific blow at Tommy's face. But Wentworth blocked the punch, pushing the chauffeur aside. He seized Tommy about the waist and effortlessly lifted his frail, struggling body from the ground.

"Lemme go!" Tommy panted. "Lemme kill him—"

Carl Webster's face was ghostly white; the whiteness of one whose cheek has just been fanned by the breath of Death. But he maintained his poise.

"Moulton!" he exclaimed. "You saved my life! Why in God's name does the boy want to kill me?"

Wentworth grimly thrust him aside and forced the still struggling newsboy into the car.

"Get in here, Webster!" he ordered harshly, "before the police come. We don't want Tommy going to jail!"

Webster obeyed. He could not do less for the one who had just pushed Death's hand aside from him.

At a nod from Webster, Mike Stockly got behind the wheel and tooled the big car away from the curb. The small crowd which had already begun to gather was left gaping on the sidewalk, not even understanding what had happened in those few fleet moments of swift action. To the patrolman, who came running over from his post across the street, in front of the Garden, they told confusing and conflicting stories. One man maintained that a newsboy had been kidnapped in the car; another said that a man in a brown suit had fired at the car, which had then jumped the curb and struck the trash can; a third maintained that five gangsters in the car had dragged a passing man into it and were taking him for a ride. The cop scratched his head in confusion. He had recognized Carl Webster's town car, and hesitated to turn in an alarm for it. So he compromised by phoning in to his precinct house and asking the desk sergeant's instructions.

In the meantime at Joe Moulton's direction, the town car was driven swiftly across the Park to Carl Webster's home just off Fifth Avenue. They hustled Tommy Tildon into the palatial house, while Mike Stockly took the car back to the garage.

CHAPTER 8
BLONDE OMEN

IN WEBSTER'S library, the newsboy suddenly broke down. He burst into tears; his thin little body was wracked by violent sobs as he clung to Wentworth, trying to blink back the tears.

Wentworth gently eased him into a chair, while Carl Webster poured a double Scotch and downed it neat.

"Phew!" he said. "I needed that! Here, Moulton, I poured one for you—"

Wentworth wanted no liquor tonight. The coming battle with Red Feather would provide all the stimulation he needed. But he took the glass and placed it to Tommy's lips, allowing the lad to sip a few drops.

"There," he said in kindly fashion. "Do you feel better now, sonny?"

Tommy Tildon looked up at him out of tear-filled eyes. There was no longer any hate in them—only deep contrition. He did not recognize Richard Wentworth in his disguise.

"Thanks, mister, for what you did," he whispered hoarsely. "I—I would have been a murderer if you hadn't stopped me!"

"But why?" demanded Carl Webster. "Why in the world did you want to kill me, Tommy?"

The lad shuddered. "You know why!" he said.

Out of his pocket he pulled a crushed and crinkled envelope. Wentworth took it, and saw that there was no stamp on it, but that it carried a superscription scrawled in pencil:

> *"Finder please deliver at once to: Tom Tildon, 890 East 49th Street."*

"Read the letter!" Tommy said hoarsely.

Wentworth glanced quickly at Carl Webster, and then extracted the single sheet which the envelope contained. It bore a short message which had evidently been written in frantic haste; perhaps in the dark, for the lines went off at all angles, and crossed each other twice, making it very difficult to decipher.

As Wentworth looked at it, Tommy, sitting with clenched hands as if trying to restrain himself, said, "That's from Lillian. She hasn't been home for two days. When I asked Mr. Webster where she was, he said he hadn't seen her, that she hadn't come to work—"

"That's right," Carl Webster broke in. "Lillian didn't show up at the office yesterday, or the day before—"

"And tonight," Tommy interrupted, "a man left this note at the house, with our landlady. The man said he'd found it in the gutter on Riverside Drive. Read it. Read it and you'll see why I tried—to kill him!" Once more there was a terrible light of hatred in the lad's eyes as he looked at Carl Webster.

Wentworth hastily put a hand on the boy's shoulder, and held the note up so that both he and Webster could read it. With difficulty they were able to understand the scrawled writing:

"Tommy dear—Red Feather has me. I've been a prisoner for two days and they've kept my eyes taped, and I'm writing this without seeing it. One of the men gave me paper and pencil because I begged him, and now they're going to take me in a car somewhere, and I hope to drop this out as we ride. Oh, Tommy, Red Feather has tortured me, and he's going to kill me. The pain all over my body is dreadful and I daren't even tell you what they've done to me. I'll never see you again, Tommy, in this world, but I must tell you what I heard the men saying—Red Feather is—Carl Webster! Don't tell the police, Red Feather will get you if you do. But watch out and be careful. I don't know why they've done this to me, I haven't any money or anything they want, and they might do it to you. For God's sake, Tommy, try to save yourself. Go away. Or try to contact the Spider. I heard the men saying that the Spider was the only one whom Red Feather feared. God forgive me, I can't believe it, but I'm sure I heard it—that Carl Webster is Red Feather...."

The writing trailed off as if she had been abruptly interrupted. There was no signature.

"That's Lillian's writing!" Tommy gulped. "I'd know it anywhere. And she says—she says—" his voice rose hysterically as his eyes lanced burning hatred at Carl Webster—"she says that *you* are Red Feather. *You* tortured her. You're going to kill her—or you've done it already!"

Carl Webster's face grew pallid as he stepped back from the lad's vitriolic outburst.

"No!" he exclaimed. "God, you mustn't believe that, Tommy! I loved Lillian as if she were my own daughter. I had great plans for her—and for you. I would never harm her." He turned pleadingly to Wentworth. "Moulton! You don't believe I'm Red Feather, do you?"

Wentworth's face was grave and puzzled. "I don't know what to believe," he said slowly. His glance dropped once more to the letter, then switched to Tommy Tildon.

"Where did you get the gun, Tommy?"

"It—it used to belong to my brother, Joe. We kept his gun and his badge after he was killed, preventing that hold-up. We also have the police medal he got—"

"If Joe were alive, Tommy, he wouldn't like to think of you as a murderer."

The boy covered his face with his hands, and gave way to unrestrained sobbing. Wentworth nodded sympathetically and took Carl Webster by the arm. He led him over to the window, so that the boy couldn't hear what he had to say.

"I TELL you, Moulton," Webster began in a hoarse whisper, "there's something fiendish going on. Poor Lillian was tortured, and then deliberately led to believe that I was Red Feather, so that she'd write that note. They even gave her a chance to write it and think that she was unobserved. Then one of Red Feather's own men must have delivered it to Tommy's home. God, what a plot—and all for the purpose of getting me killed!"

"How do you know that was the purpose?" Wentworth asked.

For answer, Carl Webster took another letter from his pocket. This one was postmarked, and addressed to Webster at his office, and had a Special Delivery stamp.

"Here," he said. "This speaks for itself."

Slowly, Wentworth took the enclosure from the envelope, and unfolded it. He stiffened as he saw the carefully drawn reproduction of a heron's feather at the top of the note. It was drawn in red ink, and looked just like the feathers that had been found beside the bodies of Red Feather's victims. The note read:

"Carl Webster:

You have the unfortunate honor to be on my list of contributors, voluntary or otherwise. The sum assigned to you is $150,000. This is little enough, considering the value of your life, and your financial resources. Your secretary, under my artful persuasion, has already given me full information as to your bank balances. She was a brave girl, and refused to talk in spite of great physical pain, so I employed a little trick, making her think that I was you. In the conversation that followed, she unwittingly divulged all the information I needed. I tell you this so that you won't think her a traitor to yourself, because I want you to remember that if you go to the police with this note, Lillian Tildon will die in a far more terrible way than planned for her. What I want you to do is to withdraw $150,000 in cash in any denominations you wish. Select an intermediary, but tell him nothing of what he must do until eleven o'clock tonight. At that time you *will give him the cash and tell him to go to Riverside Drive and One Hundred and Tenth Street, with the money in a paper parcel. My men will handle the rest. Meet this intermediary at your office at eleven o'clock sharp, and let him start out at ten minutes after eleven. In the event that you do not meet this demand, Lillian Tildon will be painfully killed, and you will die before midnight. Believe me, sir, to be earnestly yours,*

RED FEATHER."

"I see," breathed Wentworth, raising his glance to meet that of Carl Webster. "And you were going to use me as the intermediary?"

"Yes, Moulton. I knew I could trust you for the job. I have the money in the car, all wrapped and ready. But I don't understand why they set Tommy onto me before the money was paid over."

"That's easy," Wentworth said bitterly. "Red Feather intended to kill you anyway—whether you paid or not. But something must have gone wrong with his timing. Tommy got the letter from his sister before he was supposed to."

IT WAS then the phone rang. Tommy did not move, but sat with his head in his hands, though his sobs had abated somewhat. Carl Webster almost jumped at the sound of the bell. He seized the instrument and said hoarsely, "Well?"

He held the receiver well away from his ear, so that Wentworth could hear what was said at the other end.

"How do you do, Mr. Webster?" said that same cold, emotionless voice which he had heard only a little while ago over the switchboard in the West View Hotel. "I am sorry that my arrangements went a little wild. That letter should have been delivered to Tommy Tildon, *only* if you failed to pay up tonight. My agent made a mistake. Believe me, he shall be well punished. As for you, are you still ready to pay the sum specified?"

"Why, you—you—" Carl Webster's face became red and mottled with anger. "You murderous fiend! I'll pay no—"

He stopped short as Wentworth tugged at his sleeve. "Tell him you'll pay! Let me go with the money!"

Webster hesitated, and then a gleam came into his eyes. He put his mouth to the phone. "Wait, Red Feather. I've changed my mind—"

He broke off, and gave Wentworth a despairing look. "He's hung up!"

"Damn!" Wentworth whispered under his breath. This was another chance lost to contact Red Feather.

"I'm sorry, said Webster."I should have thought faster. By God, now Red Feather will try to kill me again."

A loud, persistent horn began to blast in the street, just outside the window.

Webster frowned, and ran to the window, but Wentworth pulled him back. "Don't show yourself!" he cried. "Red Feather works fast. That may be his men—"

He pulled the curtain aside and peered out. As he did so Tommy came out of his chair and stood next to Wentworth, looking out of the window. They saw a car, without headlights, at the curb directly in front of the house. The street lamp illuminated eerily the faces of the three brown men inside—one at the wheel, and two in the back. As Wentworth and Tommy watched, the door of the sedan opened, and a body was thrust out to the sidewalk. It fell with a thud, and lay still upon its back. It was the body of a blonde-haired girl, and it was entirely naked; long, bloody wounds covered the white skin. The eyes were open, staring upward under the street lamp, and the face was contorted into a frozen death mask of unutterable agony. "**OH, GOD!**" Tommy Tildon screamed.

"It's Lillian!" His voice ended in a gurgling, choked cry as he flung himself headlong through the window pane, crashing through it to land on his knees on the turf just outside. He sprang up and ran awkwardly with his crippled gait, shaking his fists at the sedan. Blood stained his face and hands where he had been cut by broken glass, and he looked like a puny but terrible figure of vengeance as he went straight for the black sedan.

Wentworth uttered a low voiced oath. His hand streaked up and down from his armpit, coming out with a gun. He started to put a leg over the sill to go after Tommy, when he felt his coat seized from behind. He was dragged back by Carl Webster, who shouted, "No, no! You'll be killed. See the machine gun—"

Wentworth pushed him violently away and started over the sill once more. But he was too late. It was not a machine gun which Webster had seen in the window of the sedan, but one those same flamethrowers which Red Feather used to such horribly effective purpose. Flame streaked from the sedan and engulfed Tommy Tildon. He threw up his hands and screamed once, terribly, and then he fell to the ground.

Wentworth, his lips drawn into a hard line, emptied his gun at the sedan. But it was already in motion, and the bullets ricocheted harmlessly from the bulletproof metal and glass. He lowered his sights and sent the last two shots at the tires, but he knew at once that it was useless. He hit the rubber with both shots. But there was no *pop*. The sedan was riding on solid tires!

In a moment the car, with its little, grinning brown men, was out of sight around the corner. And by the time Wentworth and Carl Webster got out the window, Tommy Tildon was dead. They beat out the fire in his clothes, but his frail little body was charred and black. He laid less than ten feet from the hideously mangled body of his sister, Lillian—two innocent victims of the most brilliantly vicious criminal against whom Wentworth had ever waged battle!

For a long, timeless minute, Richard Wentworth stood above the piteous body of the newsboy, forgetting that he was supposed to be Joe Moulton, forgetting everything except the burned thing at his feet.

"Tommy Tildon," he said in a voice that was strange and frightening, "I swear that you have not died in vain!"

CHAPTER 9
BATTLE IN THE CAGE

FIFTEEN MINUTES later a grim, tight-lipped man entered a drug store two blocks from Carl Webster's house, and dialed a number. People who knew Joe Moulton would have been startled to see the grimness in his face now. He had left Webster's house before the police arrived, because now less than ever did he want interference or help from Kirkpatrick or his men. He was determined to come to grips personally with the man who called himself Red Feather.

In the tragedy of the last few minutes, he had forgotten about Nita and Ram Singh. But now, after seeing a sample of Red Feather's merciless ruthlessness, he felt as if a vise were clamping at his heart as he dialed for the fourth time tonight the number of the East End Avenue apartment where he had told Nita to report.

There were now only two thin threads by which he could hope to reach contact with Red Feather: One was the cab which Nita and Ram Singh had followed from the Mallard Hotel, the other was the riddle of the *Mandalay Operation*, which he had heard Red Feather mention over the phone.

He completed dialing the code, and suddenly his blood raced as he heard the click at the other end, denoting that someone was lifting the receiver.

So Nita and Ram Singh had finally returned!

"Greeting, Master!" It was the voice of Ram Singh. "I have but just returned. Allah be praised that you called so soon—"

"Ram Singh!" Wentworth rapped. "Where is Miss Nita?"

"We followed the Onyx taxicab, Master. The cab picked up a passenger whom we do not know, and took him to a nightclub on Fifty-Ninth Street. Miss Nita followed this man into the club, and sent me hither to await your call."

"Fifty-Ninth Street? Quick, Ram Singh—the name of this club?"

"It is that club which is on the rooftop of the newly erected Steel Building, Master—"

"The Mandalay Gardens!" Wentworth barked.

"Yes, Master. Miss Nita awaits you there—"

"Ram Singh! There is great danger to Miss Nita. Red Feather plans to strike there tonight! Go there at once, Ram Singh. I will meet you in front of the building!"

"By Allah!" the Sikh growled. "Perhaps we shall have some good fighting! I go, Master!"

Wentworth hung up, and raced out of the booth. He hailed a cab and rapped out, "Mandalay Gardens!"

Grimly, as the cab rolled northward, he inserted a pair of clips in his automatics. He wanted to stop and change his appearance back to that of Richard Wentworth. But there was no time for that. He must go as Joe Moulton, gambler.

The Mandalay Gardens! Why hadn't he thought of that when he overheard Red Feather's orders? The place was the most exclusive nightclub in New York. Atop a sixty story skyscraper, it was the focal point of all wealthiest and most socially elect of the city. To the Mandalay Gardens each night, came men of power, influence and wealth; and here too came women of rare beauty and great talent—actresses, wives and mistresses of statesmen and millionaires. What a profusion of jewels and wealth there would be for the taking in such a place, by such a man as Red Feather! And when he struck, it would be with the thoroughness and the ruthless cruelty for which he had already made himself feared.

And Nita—Nita was among those gay and innocent patrons who were slated to die tonight!

"Faster, driver. Faster!" Wentworth urged.

WHEN THEY reached Columbus Circle, he threw a bill to the cabby, and leaped out of the taxi while it was still moving. Directly in front of him was the towering bulk of the huge Steel Industries Building, reaching sixty floors toward the sky. All along the curb were parked the glittering, expensive limousines of New York's Four Hundred, whose owners were enjoying the lavish entertainment and exquisite food of the Mandalay Gardens far up on the roof of the giant structure.

Short-lived indeed would be their enjoyment, for they did not know that tonight they were to receive the attentions of—Red Feather!

As Wentworth leaped from the cab, he saw his own Daimler swinging around the corner from Central Park South, with Ram Singh at the wheel. The Sikh gave no sign of recognizing Wentworth in his disguise as Joe Moulton, but merely pulled the car in to the curb in a vacant space alongside a fire plug.

Wentworth, who had already left his cab, slowed up for a moment as he passed the Daimler's open window. His swift, all embracing glance spotted a number of cars distributed at various points around Columbus Circle, which were apparently merely parked there. However, in each sat a silent man as if awaiting a signal. It was a strange thing that all of them should have chosen Columbus Circle in which to park their cars and have a quiet smoke.

"There are many who watch, Ram Singh," Wentworth said in Punjabi. "You will come up with me, but you will not appear to know me—"

"They will not let me in, Master," the Sikh said hurriedly. "Only those with cards—"

"Make some pretext, then. Say that you have brought Miss Nita's gloves—"

"And if they still refuse, Master? Shall I crack their skulls?"

"Use any means you can think of—*but be sure to come up.* Once upstairs, your task will be to locate Miss Nita, and remain at her side every instant. It is you, Ram Singh, who must protect her tonight. I shall have work...."

As he spoke he was already past the Daimler, moving into the lobby of the Steel Industries Building. An observer would not have thought that any words had passed between the flashily dressed gambler and the Sikh chauffeur in the Daimler. But almost at once, Ram Singh got out of the limousine and went swiftly into the building. He passed Wentworth, who was purposely walking more slowly, and headed straight for the special elevator which served the Mandalay Gardens. Wentworth turned aside to a phone booth, while Ram Singh entered the elevator. He could hear the Sikh arguing in a loud and belligerent voice with the Hindu doorman and with the elevator operator.

All the employees of the Mandalay Gardens were native Hindus, imported by the management for the express purpose of lending Oriental color to the nightclub. Each attendant was dressed in white turban and white burnoose, and carried a wide bladed, curved scimitar in his waistband. The scimitars, of course, were not made of steel, but of thin, shellacked wood, polished to such a high degree that they fooled many of the patrons.

It was with two of these attendants that Ram Singh had to argue in order to be permitted to go upstairs to the roof garden. The doorman tried to stop him from entering the elevator, but the huge Sikh merely pushed him to one side and stepped into the cage. The elevator operator motioned to him to get out.

"You may not go up, chauffeur. Step out—"

"*Bismillah!*" thundered Ram Singh. "You son of a dog! Will you speak to me so? I go up!" He brandished a huge roll of bills in one hand. "My mistress has sent me to fetch money for her, so that she may try her fortune at the gaming table in your Mandalay Gardens. I must bring it to her!"

The doorman came in and took him by one arm, while the elevator operator seized him by the other.

"Come now, chauffeur, get out. We will not take you up. Give us the money and we will send it to your mistress."

Ram Singh laughed deep in his chest, and with a single powerful lunge he sent both turbaned attendants staggering through the elevator door.

"What! Trust you jackals with my mistress's money? Never!"

IT WAS at that moment that Wentworth emerged from the phone booth. He had made a single quick call to Commissioner Kirkpatrick.

His message was short. With the deep, metallic voice he knew so well how to use, he had said, "Kirkpatrick, this is the Spider! Wait! Say nothing, but listen closely, for there is no time. Men and women are going to die at any moment. You have often said that the Spider should cooperate with the police. Well, this is my answer. Send men—many men, quickly, to the Mandalay Gardens. Red Feather plans a raid!"

"When?" Kirkpatrick rapped.

"I don't know. Perhaps it will be in an hour, perhaps in five minutes, perhaps in one minute. God grant your men come in time. I shall be there—in case they are late!"

"Wait, Spider!" Kirkpatrick's voice came harsh and unyielding over the wire. "If your tip is authentic, then I thank you. If through your information we are enabled to capture Red Feather it will be a great boon to the city. But—I warn you—there is no reprieve for you. You are still wanted. If you are at the Mandalay Gardens when I arrive, you shall be captured—dead or alive. I want that clearly understood!"

"I ask no favors of you, Kirkpatrick!" Wentworth said coldly.

And with that, without giving Kirkpatrick a chance to ask another question, Wentworth hung up and hurried out to the elevator cage. He was just in time to see the doorman and the operator come hurtling out on to the lacquered floor, propelled there by Ram Singh's powerful thrust.

Before the two turbaned men could recover their footing, Wentworth seized each by the scruff of the neck and thrust them violently back into the cage.

Another party of men and women in evening clothes was just entering, and Wentworth closed the door of the cage before these new arrivals could catch a glimpse of what was going on. Then he pushed over the lever and sent the cage shooting upward.

The two turbaned men were scrambling to their feet, the

make-believe scimitars having fallen from their waistbands. But weapons suddenly appeared in their hands—gleaming knives, with which they leaped upon Wentworth and Ram Singh!

For a long second the elevator cage shot upward without a guiding hand as Wentworth turned to defend himself against the onslaught. He caught his man's descending knife hand, twisted the wrist in a quick, deft *jiu-jitsu* maneuver, and the blade went flying out of the man's grip accompanied by a screech of pain.

Ram Singh handled his man with less finesse but with just as much efficiency. He uttered a roar of glee, and charged directly into the attacker.

In the close quarters of the elevator cage, they were all thrust against each other, and Ram Singh's attacker backed away from the Sikh's bull lunge, only to bump into his companion, who was still screeching with the pain of his twisted wrist.

Ram Singh shouted in Punjabi: *"Bismillali!* I kill jackals!"

His huge, hairy hands flicked out, fingers wrapping themselves around each man's throat. Then, with hardly the sign of exertion on his part, he brought the two of them together with a crash. Their heads met with pile driver force, and the two men went limp. Ram Singh dropped them carelessly to the floor.

"Wah!" he grunted. "Pigs like these should not seek a quarrel with fighting men!"

Wentworth was already back at the controls, his forehead was wrinkled.

"I don't like it, Ram Singh. These two are no ordinary attendants. Otherwise they would not have knives."

Ram Singh spat contemptuously. "I hope that this Red Feather will give us worthier foemen than these before the night is over!"

"I'm afraid," Wentworth said soberly, "that your wish will be granted!"

CHAPTER 10
RED FEATHER
DEMONSTRATES

THEIR CAR was an express elevator, and there was no stop before the sixtieth floor. Blank walls faced them all the way up. But when the indicator showed "60," strains of exotic music filtered through. "Prelude to Terror" might have been an appropriate title for the selection, Wentworth thought, as the cage came to rest at the top floor. He opened the sliding door and motioned to Ram Singh, who stepped out quickly. Wentworth followed, deftly closing the door behind him so that those on the floor might not see the two unconscious men in the cage.

The entire top floor of the building was devoted to service space for the Mandalay Gardens on the roof above. The foyer into which Wentworth and Ram Singh stepped had no doubt cost many thousands of dollars to furnish. Rich Baluchistan rugs cushioned the sound of their footsteps, and oriental drapes of untold value hung from ceiling to floor on all the walls. There was a great curving staircase which led from here up to a mezzanine, from which in turn, a smaller flight took the patrons out into the roof garden.

Down here on this floor were the kitchens and the bar, as well as dressing rooms for the patrons. Also, at one end of the floor, and well protected from the casual approach of any but the initiated, was the gambling hall where men and women of the elite could play for stakes as high as fifty thousand dollars.

Everywhere there was bustle and activity. Waiters hurried back and forth, and beautiful women in evening clothes emerged from the dressing rooms to meet their escorts who were waiting for them at the foot of the grand staircase.

Wentworth had never been able to discover just who owned the Mandalay Gardens. But whoever it was must surely have a fortune at his disposal, for the lavish furnishings and the expensive service and cuisine represented an overhead expenditure that the owner couldn't possibly hope to get back out of the patrons. For no matter how much they charged for a bottle of champagne or a caviar sandwich, it was manifestly impossible to make a profit. The exclusive social set who frequented the Mandalay Gardens assumed that it was supported *sub rosa*, by one of their own set, who probably had nothing to do with his money but amuse himself.

All the waiters were swarthy men, attired in white turbans, but instead of the burnoose, they wore pantaloons and tight fitting, sleeveless jackets of embroidered cloth. The attendant who was charged with the duty of welcoming guests as they came off the elevator was a tall, dark-skinned girl, who wore nothing but a tight fitting, spangled band about her breasts, and a pair of diaphanous silk pantaloons. At the head of the stairs, leading out into the Mandalay Gardens itself, stood the head-waiter, who was attired like an Indian Rajah.

The hostess in the silk pantaloons frowned at Ram Singh and Wentworth. "All guests must wear evening clothes!"

Ram Singh pushed past her and started for the staircase. "I will stay but a minute, sweet girl," he grinned at her, showing two rows of gorgeously white teeth through his beard. "I must see my mistress for a moment. The one who guards the door down below has not stopped me, as you see."

The girl shrugged, and let him pass. After all, it was none of her business. If the doorman had allowed this chauffeur up, then it must be all right. She turned to Wentworth, and frowned again. For he was no longer there!

The soft, indirect lighting left the whole place in a sort of semi darkness, which was conducive to the atmosphere of eastern luxury with which the place was imbued. But it was also conducive to the swift and unperceived movements of the dark, shadowy figure in the black cloak and hat, which seemed to blend with the shadows as he disappeared into the alcove recesses of the restrooms....

THE DARK-SKINNED hostess wrinkled her forehead. "I wonder where that man in the tan suit went—"

She very quickly forgot about the man in the tan suit, for her attention was attracted to the head of the grand staircase where a vehement argument had begun between the bearded Sikh in the chauffeur's uniform, and the headwaiter in the robes of a rajah.

"Impossible!" The head-waiter was gesticulating wildly. "You cannot go in there. It would be sacrilege! Imagine—a chauffeur entering the dining room of the Mandalay Gardens!"

"Nevertheless," Ram Singh said silkily, "that is where I go, my pig!"

He pushed past the headwaiter that snatched at the jacket of Ram Singh's uniform, and shouted for help.

Half a dozen turbaned attendants came running up the stairs to his aid. And strangely enough, they drew those scimitars of theirs, which they carried in their waist bands. As they came up they brandished them. And the blades glittered as no wood ever glitters, no matter how highly it is polished or shellacked. Those scimitars were real, deadly weapons, made of steel. And these turbaned men were no mere attendants, but Hindu killers!

In a glance Ram Singh realized all this, and he suddenly laughed deep in his throat. The head waiter was still clutching at his coat when he whirled around in a single lithe motion, and picked up the head waiter as if he had been no more than a child. Then, with the superb ease of smooth and powerful muscles trained to perform any task asked of them, Ram Singh hurled his assailant directly straight at the advancing Hindus!

The man screeched, and his arms flailed the air wildly. His body struck the group of Hindus with the force of an avalanche, and sent them all rolling back down the grand staircase like a batch of ninepins.

At the top of the stairs Ram Singh threw out his chest, and, showing both rows of white, even teeth, laughed loudly. He waved a hand ironically to the red-faced head waiter who was

Blagg went flying through space—his hands clawing at thin air!

getting to his feet, but was all tangled up in the folds of his rajah's robe.

"*Allah, akbar!*" he sang out to the sweating group below, speaking to them in Hindustani. "Ye are no true Moslems. Ye are carrion, and pig eaters. When I return, ye carrion, I will show you how a True Believer fights!"

And so saying, Ram Singh turned on his heel and went through the door at the head of the stairs, which led out to the Mandalay Gardens.

The orchestra was playing a soft and slumberous Oriental melody, and a girl upon a raised dais was dancing a sensuous eastern dance whose every movement was calculated to arouse the passions of men. The dancer wore no single bit of clothing. Her body was oiled from head to foot, so that she glistened in the amber spotlight. Her hair was black in two great braids behind her. Fingernails and toenails were painted a vivid red so that they shone like scars against the background of her brown and oily skin. And every eye in the room was turned upon her in unhealthy fascination.

It was exhibitions such as these which brought the blasé social set to the Mandalay Gardens. They had thought that nothing could thrill them any more—till they came and witnessed the exotic numbers presented here. Upon the tables the food and drink lay unnoticed while all followed the strange and provoking dance.

Ram Singh's eyes only flickered to the dancer. For a second they lingered upon her, appreciatively. And then the Sikh was all business again. For him there was a time and a place for everything. Now was not the time for pleasures of the flesh.

HIS GLANCE darted all over the room, and finally centered upon Nita van Sloan, sitting alone at a table near the edge of the roof garden. He looked behind him to make sure that the Hindus were not pursuing him, and grinned when he saw the headwaiter eyeing him murderously from the doorway. They would not dare to come after him out here, for the slightest disturbance would break the spell of that voluptuous dance.

He crossed the floor toward his mistress, and no one even noticed him or his chauffeur's uniform—so rapt was their attention upon the dancer silhouetted in the amber spotlight.

But Nita saw him. Perhaps she alone of all that gay throng had eyes for anything else. She was sitting tense and watchful, though none but the Sikh could have noticed anything unusual about her.

As soon as he was at her table, she raised her eyes to his, questioningly.

"Master Dick?"

Ram Singh smiled, and nodded. "He is here, Mistress Nita."

Her body relaxed, and a little sigh of relief escaped from her lips.

Ram Singh went through the motions of handing her the money which he was supposed to be bringing her. Under his breath he said, "Be careful, Mistress Nita. There are many who watch us. And here comes one whom I like not!"

Nita turned slightly to look at the tall man with the gaunt,

99

skeletal face, whom she remembered having seen last, in the cocktail lounge of the Mallard Hotel.

He threw a quick look of distaste at Ram Singh, then turned to Nita and bowed from the hips. "Permit me, mademoiselle. I have the honor to present myself—Baron Cornelius Crispi. It is my privilege to be a friend of the management here. They have asked me to speak with you. This chauffeur of yours—it is impossible to allow him to remain. You understand—the other patrons…."

"Of course," said Nita. She looked up at Ram Singh. "You had better go now—"

The Sikh moved deliberately around the table until he was standing behind the chair which faced her. His back was now to the dais upon which the dancer was performing. He drew himself up to his full height, and folded his arms over his chest.

"It is my great sorrow that I must disobey, Mistress Nita. I have my orders. The Master has ordered that I remain at your side until you arrive home. I must stay."

Nita frowned. She looked up at Baron Crispi with a little helpless gesture. "You see, Baron, it is quite impossible for me to order him to leave. He won't go."

Crispi's face was utterly expressionless. For a long minute he stared at Ram Singh. Then he looked down at Nita.

"It is too bad," he said. Then he bowed once more from the hips, turned on his heel, and strode away.

Nita glanced up at the Sikh. "Watch where he goes, Ram Singh!"

"I watch, Mistress," he said, in Punjabi. "It is he whom we

followed here. I have the thought that he is one who can be a dangerous enemy!"

Nita said, "Ram Singh! I am afraid of that man. He—he looks like Death itself."

The Sikh smiled. "Have no fear, Mistress. The Master is close by. And while I am beside thee, they must kill *me* before they can touch thee—" Something whined past Nita's ear, like the low hum of a distant bee. And Ram Singh ceased speaking, with a dreadful, appalling suddenness.

His body stiffened as that same something which had whined in the air, struck him in the chest. Blood spurted from a wound high above his heart, and the bone handle of a long bladed, glittering knife vibrated in the wound. Someone had thrown the knife from the shadows, and it had struck true to the mark. RAM SINGH'S teeth tightened upon his lower lip, and he slowly raised both hands to the knife handle. He wavered on his feet, and his forehead became bathed in perspiration. Slowly, painfully, he tried to pull the knife out. His great body seemed to heave in a mighty, titanic struggle against the wicked wound.

"Mistress Nita!" he gasped. "Guard thyself! Thy unworthy servant—has—failed thee!"

And he toppled over with a crash.

As if that had been a signal, the music suddenly ceased. Dead silence fell upon the Mandalay Gardens. The dancer came to a rigid stop, poised with her arms in the air. For a full two seconds, it seemed as if nobody breathed.

And then a shrill whistle pierced the night air. The dancer bent low in a sort of crouch, and ran from the dais through the curtains at the rear, her brown, oiled flanks glistening under the amber light.

And then the spotlight went out. For an instant, the roof garden was plunged into utter darkness.

Nita van Sloan was on her knees, cradling the head of Ram Singh, who was bleeding on the floor. When the light went out, she could not see his bearded, pain wracked face any more. But she heard his gurgling voice: *"Go, Mistress. Go quickly. Guard yourself. Leave me—"*

"No, Ram Singh!" There were tears in her eyes, and her words choked in her throat. "I—I'll stay with you."

She felt the Sikh's head jerk against her breast, as from somewhere in the darkness, a cold, emotionless voice began to speak. The voice was coming from a concealed loudspeaker, and it dominated that whole roof garden with a sort of fiendish malevolence.

"Listen, all of you! You are hearing the words of Red Feather! Many of you have heard from me privately. You have been ordered to do certain things. *I will now show you what happens to those who disobey!"*

Abruptly, the amber spotlight went on once more, flooding the dais. Upon the platform there was a wooden rack, some six feet high and five feet wide. Spread-eagled within the frame of that rack was the body of a girl. Wrists and ankles were stretched taut by ropes tied to the framework. Her head hung limp upon her breast, but her face was etched by the spotlight, as was the rest of her body. A great gasp went up from all those who were sitting, paralyzed by fright, at the tables. They all knew that dead girl.

"Ellen Blount!" the name whipped around the garden, from table to table.

Every eye was fixed upon that pitiful victim. And it was easy to see what had been done to her. For it was apparent that there was not a whole bone left in the body. While she was stretched taut upon the rack, she had been struck repeatedly with a hammer or a heavy bar, each blow breaking another bone. How long that inhuman torture had lasted while she yet lived, no one could tell.

Women began to scream hysterically; men cursed in low, subdued voices. Nita van Sloan, with Ram Singh's bearded head against her breast, gasped with horror. And as suddenly as the amber spot had gone on, it now went out.

A hush spread over the garden.

At once, Red Feather's voice came again, "The girl you just saw was the daughter of Irene Blount. I ordered Irene Blount to perform a certain task. She thought to cheat me, by killing herself instead of doing the thing I ordered. She thought that if she were dead, I would spare her daughter. Well, you have all seen how wrong she was. I promised Irene Blount that her daughter would be broken bone by bone until dead, unless my will was done. And that has happened. Remember, all of you— you cannot escape the will of Red Feather, even by destroying yourselves!"

CHAPTER 11
TRAP FOR THE SPIDER!

WHILE THAT cold and heartless voice was proceeding, a shadow which was darker than all the other shadows upon the roof seemed to move around behind the dais like an oozing puddle of blackness. This shadowy figure seemed to be interested not in the voice, nor in the dais, nor even in any of those present. It seemed to be tracing wires. Could anyone have noticed that dark blotch in the night, it would have appeared to be nothing more than the shadow of one of the palms. In reality, it was a man; a man whose features were hidden by the night and by the brim of a black slouch hat; whose deft hands were covered by black gloves, and whose entire form was enveloped by a cloak darker than the night.

This figure at last seemed to find what it sought, for it bent and touched a wire which ran along one side of the roof, up against the trellised coping. Swiftly it followed that wire toward the rear. This was the cable connecting the loudspeaker with the microphone into which Red Feather was talking. The loudspeaker was hidden under the dais. And by following the wire, the black-cloaked figure would come to the microphone.

The voice of Red Feather continued.

"And now you shall all of you contribute to the war chest of Red Feather. When the lights go on, my men will circulate among you. You will strip yourselves of your jewels, your diamonds, and your money. Put everything into the sacks my men carry. I warn you, hold nothing back. My eyes will be on you. Whoever holds back will die on the instant!"

With the last word, the lights went on all over the place.

The body of the dead girl, Ellen Blount, still hung upon the rack, a gruesome reminder of the heartless cruelty of Red Feather.

And from all sides, came small brown men. Like the attendants and the waiters, they were clad in white turbans and burnooses. Each had a scimitar at his belt, and an open sack in his hand. For each man with an open sack, there was another at his side with a queer, bell shaped gun, whose stock resembled a bellows.

The brown men began to circulate among the tables. They spoke no single word, but merely stood with the yawning sacks while a roomful of trembling men and women poured jewels and money into them.

The shadowy figure had faded back against the trellised coping along the side of the roof garden. From under the low hat brim, glittering eyes stabbed in all directions, seeking, seeking, seeking... Somewhere here, Red Feather was hidden. He had said that he could see everything. Therefore he himself must be within sight.

And suddenly, that vague shadow seemed to stiffen. The glittering eyes were fixed upon the water tower, high above the roof. A wire ran down from that structure, to be lost in the thick climbing ivy of the trelliswork. It ran to the top of the water tower, where there was a small cupola, apparently placed there for decoration, but which was large enough to hold a man comfortably.

The little brown men were making the rounds methodically. Two of them came to the table where Nita van Sloan had been sitting. She was on the floor, still cradling Ram Singh's head against her breast. She stared up defiantly at the two small brown men.

Just then a scream sounded from the other end of the garden. It diverted their attention from Nita. Over at the end from which the scream had come, a woman in evening clothes was cowering away from one of the turbaned killers.

The brown man had ripped away the front of the dress, and was pointing to a string of pearls which she had tried to hide from him.

And from above came the cold voice of Red Feather. "Woman, I warned you. You must pay the penalty!"

At once, one of the brown men with the bellows gun turned it upon the unfortunate woman. Before he could squeeze the bellows, however, a single shot blasted from somewhere in the darkness. The man screamed, and toppled backward, dropping the bellows gun. At once, all the other brown men turned in the direction from which the shot had come. They beheld a figure of vengeance rising out of the shadows. Cloaked and terrible, it belched flame from two thundering guns, and as they blasted, brown men fell everywhere.

BUT THERE were many of them, and new ones came, with bellows guns. They squeezed, and flame lanced out across the garden toward the cloaked figure. Long, brilliant fingers of flame licked at his cloak.

And then he was no longer there, and the flames were licking at empty space.

The whole garden was thrown into a vast pandemonium of panic and fire. Men and women ran in wild fright, to escape the lancing flame from those bellows-guns, which the brown men were turning in every direction in a vicious effort once more to locate the Spider.

Had they thought of looking up at the water tower, they would have found their man. He was already up the ladder, and climbing on the far side of the tower, toward the cupola.

Somewhere down in the bowels of the building a police whistle was shrilling as Kirkpatrick's police arrived on the scene.

Fire set by the bellows guns was breaking out in half a dozen places. A woman's dress caught fire, and she raised her voice in piercing, inhuman shrieks. A man in evening clothes attempted to leap to her aid and put the fire out, but one of the brown men turned a jet of fire on him, too, and flames burst from his clothes. Now, all those wealthy patrons were milling about in stark terror, and the brown men ran among them snatching jewels, rings, necklaces. They did not seem to be worried or hurried by the approach of the police.

Far up on the top of the water-tower, a desperate, deadly battle to the death was going on.

The Spider had managed to reach the top, by using the ladder which ran up along the side. And just as he put his hand on the top rung, a man emerged from the cupola. One single glance at the face of this man, which was illuminated by the flames from below, told the Spider that he had failed once more to run Red Feather to earth.

This man was not Red Feather. It was the flat-nosed Blagg.

Bitterly, the Spider understood that Red Feather had been too clever and too cautious to endanger himself up there in the water tower cupola. He had sent another to make his speech, imitating that cold, hard voice.

But there was no time for regrets. Blagg bent over the top of the water tower, his flat-nosed face peering down at the caped figure of the Spider. A gleam of vicious triumph entered his eyes. No doubt he saw here a golden opportunity to earn a rich reward from his master by ending the career of the Spider.

His hand, gripping a gun, pushed over the edge of the water tower, pointblank in the Spider's face. But before he could pull the trigger, the Spider's free hand had reached up and caught his ankle, yanking hard.

Blagg went over backward, uttering a wild shout. The gun flew from his hand as he hit the roof of the water tower. He scrambled to his knees, swung around—and came face to face with the Spider, who had vaulted up alongside him.

Blagg shouted hoarsely, and leaped at the cloaked figure. His courage was that of a cornered rat. There was no retreat from the top of the water tower except by jumping. And to jump from this side was to drop sixty floors out into space. So, with the rat-like bravery of a beast that had been run to earth, he bared his teeth and threw himself upon the Spider.

The two men grappled there on the water tower roof sixty

floors above *terra firma*, and their bodies strained as they strove to break each other's grips. Blagg had one hand about the Spider's throat, and with the other he was gouging for his eyes.

The Spider reached up with both hands and seized the one arm of Blagg, then turned swiftly with his back to the flat-nosed man. Too late, Blagg understood the maneuver. He tried desperately to break that hold, and screamed shrilly when he failed. The next moment, the Spider had heaved him over his caped back, and Blagg went flying through space—hands clawing at thin air. The sound that issued from his lips was like that of nothing human. And then his body went hurdling into the vast darkness beyond the building—out, out into space, turning over and over on itself until it disappeared from view.

FOR A long minute the Spider stood very still, waiting to hear the thud of the falling body against one of the setbacks below. But there was no thud. Evidently he had thrown the man far enough out so that he fell clear of the building, all the way down to the ground.

Swiftly now, the Spider reloaded his two automatics and went to the edge of the tower. He frowned as he looked down. Fire was raging in half a dozen places. Men and women were milling around, trampling each other in attempts to escape. But of the little brown men with the bellows guns, there was not a sign. They had made good their escape. But how? Surely, not down through the building, for the police were on their way up.

Anxiously, the Spider's gaze scanned that throng, seeking Nita. Ram Singh was there, lying on his back by the table, with the blood soaking into his tunic. But Nita was not beside him.

And the Spider knew her well enough to know that she would not have deserted the wounded Sikh of her own free will!

With reckless speed, the cloaked figure descended the ladder and sped through the hysterical crowd to the side of Ram Singh. People made way for him with awe and fear—albeit, they had seen him espouse their cause against the little brown men. They let him pass without touching him, and he stooped quickly alongside the Sikh.

"Ram Singh!" he said with a catch in his throat. "They got you, my friend!"

A tired smile showed through the Sikh's bearded lips. "No, no, Master, do not think of me, who am an unworthy servant. They have taken Mistress Nita. Go. Go quickly and take her back from them. *Allah*—they will break her bones upon the rack—like that other one…."

Ram Singh's voice died away, and his head drooped, almost touching the bone handle of the knife still protruding from his chest.

The Spider bent his head close to Ram Singh's mouth, and felt a slight puff of breath. The faithful Sikh was still alive. If he could be gotten to a hospital….

The Spider laid the bearded head gently on the floor, and came erect.

And at the same instant a stream of police came storming up the grand staircase and into the garden!

At their head was Commissioner Stanley Kirkpatrick, with a gun in his hand.

Kirkpatrick saw the charred bodies of the man and the

110

woman whose clothes had caught fire, both were now still, after their agony. He saw the terrible, broken body of Ellen Blount upon the rack on the dais. He saw the dead brown men whom the Spider had shot, and he saw the flames licking at the trellis walls and the furniture. But his glance remained on none of those things for more than the space of a second. He had eyes only for one thing in that whole dreadful scene—the figure of the Spider!

Of a sudden, his face had become ten years older, and there was a gray look of agony in his fine eyes. This was the moment for which Stanley Kirkpatrick had hoped for many years. But it was also a moment which he dreaded more than anything else in life. His one tireless objective always was to catch the Spider. And here was the Spider, trapped on a rooftop, with no means of escape except a jump to his death. Kirkpatrick should have been satisfied. Yet he dreaded the moment when that hideous disguise would be stripped from the face of the Spider to reveal—he feared—the face of his dearest friend, Richard Wentworth.

CHAPTER 12
WENTWORTH'S FIRST MASTER

S LOWLY, ALMOST as if he were doing it against his will, Stanley Kirkpatrick moved forward, his gun centered on the cloaked figure.

"Spider," he said in a hoarse voice, "you are under arrest. I call on you to surrender!"

The Spider moved carefully away from the inert form of Ram

Singh, so that if there should be any shooting, the Sikh would not be hit. He brought his gloved hands out from under the cloak, and extended them, with the fists clenched.

"Handcuffs?" he asked ironically. Kirkpatrick kept him covered, never removing his eyes from the Spider's face.

"Cole!" he ordered one of his detectives. "Put the bracelets on that man!" Flames were licking here and there fitfully, and bodies lay upon the floor. Frightened men and women herded together, watching this tense scene of drama, knowing they were witnessing what had hitherto been dreamed impossible—the capture of the Spider.

A woman in the crowd moaned. "Oh, how terrible. And he helped us. He saved us all from being burned by those brown men!"

Kirkpatrick's face was gray and drawn. He watched Detective Cole approach the Spider with the glittering steel of handcuffs. The Spider's wrists were still extended. Cole approached gingerly, reaching for one of the extended wrists.

And it was then that the Spider opened his clenched left hand. It contained a small vial. He flipped the vial with his thumb, straight past Detective Cole, toward Commissioner Kirkpatrick. At the same time he opened his right hand and flipped another vial at Cole.

Both Kirkpatrick and Cole ducked instinctively. And then the vials struck the floor and shattered in a hundred pieces.

A dozen policemen fired simultaneously at the spot where the Spider had been. But the black-cloaked figure was already in motion, and the slugs ploughed through empty air.

The detectives never had a chance for another shot, because the dense, opaque clouds of Spider *Gas* rose in such thick, billowy waves that they lost sight of him behind that smoke-screen.

Kirkparick's voice rose in an angry shout: "Cover the door! Surround the roof! Spread out! Don't let him get away!"

A rush of heavy feet thundered across the roof as the police hastened to obey staccato orders. But they were running about blindly, unable to see through the thick screen of smoke that enveloped them. They barged into each other, grappled with each other thinking they had the Spider, and swore luridly when they found they were struggling with a brother officer.

And already the Spider was at the edge of the roof. With swift, deft fingers, he unwound a length of the Web from under his cloak. Working swiftly, yet with no lost motion, he tied the free end of the Web to one of the struts of the water tower. Then, with the rest of the line still wound around his body, he climbed over the roof coping, and let himself drop. He hung suspended in air thus, sixty floors above the ground, while the blinded police raced about the roof in frantic search for him. Slowly then, with both hands gripping the line, he paid it out, rolling over and over in the air so as to unwind it from around his body. His hands gripped that line tightly. If he let go for an instant, his body would go catapulting into space, whirling around as the Web unwound, just like a spool of thread that had been dropped. But the marvelous reserve power which he could always call upon in emergency enabled him to keep a firm grip on the line, paying it out foot by foot.

SLOWLY HE moved lower in space, passing the top floor window, and then coming abreast of a window in the fifty-ninth floor. Here he stopped. He pulled back his right foot and kicked, smashing the glass in the window. Then he let go the line with one hand, and caught hold of the frame. He pulled himself in through the window, and dropped to the floor of the office.

Swiftly now he produced a small knife. One of the blades was a small, fine-toothed saw. He used this to saw through the Web, for there was no means of releasing the upper end which was tied to the water tower strut. He would have to leave that much for the police to find. And nothing but that saw-toothed blade would have been sufficient to cut through the Web.

As he sped swiftly through the closed and deserted office to the corridor, he could hear the clamor from above as the police still searched for him up there.

Upstairs, he had left Ram Singh, perhaps dying of a chest wound. Somewhere in the city, Nita was in the hands of Red Feather—facing the ghastly prospect of being broken on the rack, like poor Ellen Blount. And with it all, there was the problem of how Red Feather and his little brown men had been able to leave that roof and escape from the police!

That last question was answered almost at once as he rounded a bend in the dimly lit and deserted corridor. The bank of elevators serving these floors was here, and opposite them the fire stairs. The safety door to the fire stairs was open. And straight across the tiled floor from that open safety door to the closed door of one of the elevator shafts, there was a fresh trail of blood!

This was undoubtedly the way the killers had come!

Perhaps one of the little brown men, who had been wounded in the fight upstairs had escaped this way with the others. Mentally measuring the corridor, Wentworth decided that the fire stairs were directly in line with the kitchen on the sixtieth floor. From that kitchen up there, serving elevators would run up to the roof, so that waiters could come and go for the orders. It must have been by those serving elevators that the brown men and Red Feather had escaped. Then, while the police were rushing up to the roof, the killers had come down the fire stairs and gone all the way down in an elevator previously left at this floor. Looking at the indicator on the elevator shaft before which the bloodstain laid; Wentworth saw that it showed the cage to be down at the second sub basement. In these huge buildings there were four or five basements and sub cellars, and often there were exits from them into the subway and sewage systems. Thus, the killers could easily have escaped under the very noses of the police.

And Nita must have been brought this way, too.

Grimly, Wentworth nodded as he understood why Nita had not been killed up there on the spot. Alive and a hostage, she was far more valuable to Red Feather than dead. Red Feather had forced Irene Blount to do his will by threatening the torture of her daughter. No doubt he had compelled many others to commit criminal acts by the same threat. Perhaps Arnold Metz had been forced to take those funds from his bank for the same reason.

And by the same token, Red Feather would be certain that the Spider could be brought under his thumb through Nita.

The devilish part of it was that it was entirely true. Wentworth could never allow the things to be done to Nita which had been done to Ellen Blount. Much sooner would he offer up his own life in exchange.

THE WHOLE grisly picture was clear to Wentworth in a flash as he stripped off the cloak, hat and gloves of the Spider, and stood once more in the personality of Joe Moulton.

Swiftly he sought some way of leaving the building. There was one tenuous thread by which he might still pull back onto the trail of Red Feather. That thread was Arnold Metz. The man must be questioned, forced to talk. Perhaps—even though he himself knew little about Red Feather—something he might say would give Wentworth the needed clue.

But to leave the building now was no simple matter. Even as Joe Moulton, he would most certainly be stopped if he were seen. Without doubt the police would hold and question every man and woman found in the building. If he could get an elevator up here, he might be able to shoot down to one of the sub basements and escape that way, into the subway. But all the cages were downstairs....

With a start, Wentworth whirled, and a gun appeared in his hand as if by magic. From the open safety door behind him had come the unmistakable sound of a quickly indrawn breath!

His eyes probed into the darkness of the landing beyond the door, but he saw nothing. He took a quick step forward, and sprang through the doorway, then stopped short, sucking in his breath.

A girl was crouching there. She was naked, and her body

glistened with oil. Her little hands were up pathetically before her breasts, and she looked at Wentworth with a strange and curious terror in her dark and frightened eyes. It was the dancer who had been performing under the amber spotlight when Red Feather interrupted the proceedings.

"You poor thing!" Wentworth said gently.

From an inner pocket he once more took the rubber Spider's cape. He turned it inside out, with the purple lining outward, and put it across her shoulders. She shivered and pulled it together, looking up at him gratefully.

Wentworth put out a hand and helped her to her feet. She was shivering as if with fever, and sobbing with short, jerking sobs. He put an arm around her shoulders, and she suddenly broke down and buried her dark head against his chest. Now the sobs came unrestrainedly, wracking her lithe young body.

Time was growing too short. At any moment the police would discover the fire stairs, and come barging down. Yet Wentworth let her sob without restraint for a full minute before he spoke.

"Tell me about it," he said, lifting up her chin with a finger. "You look so young. Too young to have been doing a dance like that. Were you forced to do it?"

"Y-yes," she said. "Red Feather kidnapped me. He—he told father that he'd impale me on a bed of spikes if father didn't raise two hundred thousand dollars. Father didn't have the money, so he stole it from the bank."

"You're Arnold Metz's daughter?" Wentworth asked gently. She nodded. "I'm Susan—Metz."

"But why the dance?" Wentworth asked. "How did Red Feather force you to dance?"

THE GIRL'S voice broke a little, but she went on. "When father stole the money, the police went after him. Red Feather told me he knew where father was hiding out. He said he'd betray him to the police if I didn't dance here. I—I consented. Father had made himself a thief for my sake. Could I do less for him?"

"Brave girl!" said Wentworth. His eyes were grim and bleak. "So Red Feather used the daughter to ruin the father, and the father to ruin the daughter! That's how he managed to get such sensational entertainment for the Mandalay Gardens!" His voice took on an edge of intensity. "Tell me, Susan—*do you know who Red Feather is?*"

"No," she breathed. "There are several managers, and they keep changing all the time. I—I was frightened, I hid when they showed poor Ellen Blount's body on the rack. And they forgot me when they made their escape. I followed them down, hoping I could escape—"

"Wait!" Wentworth clapped a hand suddenly over her mouth, and jerked her back through the doorway onto the landing. He had noticed just in time that one of the elevator cages was shooting up from the main floor. And the indicator stopped with startling suddenness at fifty-nine—the floor they were on!

He had barely managed to get Susan back out of sight when the shaft door slid open, and two plainclothes detectives stepped out with guns in their hands.

Susan Metz started to tremble violently in Wentworth's arms.

"They know we're here!" she whispered. "They've come for us!"

Again he put a hand over her mouth, dragged her back farther into the shadows.

In a moment however, they were reassured by the conversation of the two detectives. It was apparent from what they said that they were merely making a routine search of every floor in the building. Apparently other cages were taking other detectives to all the floors.

"I'll take this end, Mike, and you take the other," one of them said. "Shoot if you see anything. The boss says if you see the Spider, plug him!"

"Okay, Sam," Mike replied.

Wentworth and Susan heard Mike's footsteps moving away toward the end of the hall, while Sam went in the other direction.

Abruptly, Sam's footsteps stopped, close to the fire door.

Wentworth grew taut. He knew that Sam had spotted the bloodstains on the floor. He pushed Susan behind him, and stepped closer to the door.

Sam began to move again. He was stepping softly, and he was moving toward the door behind which Wentworth crouched. Wentworth saw a gun push through the doorway, then an arm. Sam was taking no chances. He was coming in with his gun in front of him.

Wentworth drew a deep breath. He thrust forth both hands, and seized the detective's arm. He yanked, and Sam came tumbling forward. Wentworth brought up his right fist to connect with the detective's jaw, and Sam crumpled. Wentworth

119

caught his sagging body, and let it down easily to the floor. His eyes glittered as he took Susan by the arm and led her swiftly across the hall into the elevator.

He slid the door shut and sent the cage rushing downward.

The express elevator shot down like a plummet, and Susan Metz gasped for breath.

Wentworth streaked past the main floor, the arcade, the first basement and the sub basement. He stopped at the lowest level, the second sub cellar.

All was dark down here as he opened the door of the cage and led Susan out.

"We've got to hurry," he told her. "The detectives on the main floor will have seen the indicator drop, and they'll know someone came down here. They'll be right on our heels!"

USING HIS flashlight, he led her through passage after passage of damp and musty concrete. He stopped at a ventilator grating, through which the rumble of a subway train was plainly audible.

"Stand back!" he ordered.

When she was sufficiently far away, he took out one of his automatics and fired seven times in quick succession into the frame bar of the grating where it was set in the concrete. The bullets ricocheted, and flying bits of cement struck all about him. The cellar was filled with the ear-splitting detonations which reverberated in wave after wave of deafening thunder.

But Wentworth was already pulling at the grating with all the strength he could muster. It loosened at the spot into which he had fired, and the metal frame began to come away from the concrete.

Susan came up close to him and whispered, "Hurry. I heard an elevator door slam back there. Someone is coming!"

Wentworth grasped the grating in both hands and braced his feet against the concrete. The muscles bulged against his tight fitting coat as he pulled with all the power he could muster.

Now he could clearly hear the sound of cautious footsteps down the other end of the sub cellar.

He clamped his teeth shut, and put every ounce of reserve into the task. And suddenly there was a crackling sound. Concrete crumbled all along the side of the frame, and the grating came away in his hands!

He seized Susan's arm and half dragged, half pushed her through the opening.

"The subway!" she exclaimed as they got out on the other side.

They were in the tunnel, and the lights of a station blinked a hundred yards away. A train was rumbling toward them, and they flattened themselves against the wall.

The train roared past like a terrible prehistoric monster, and the great rush of air in its wake almost dragged them off the ledge on to the third rail.

"Come on!" Wentworth shouted. He took her hand and began to run, with Susan hanging on behind. As the rumble of the train died away, they could hear a man in the sub cellar they had left, shouting to them to stop.

Wentworth turned and saw a uniformed policeman leveling a gun at them.

He yanked Susan off the ledge, hurdling the third rail, just as the patrolman fired. The shot made a queer, whining sound in the subway tunnel, like the wailing of a banshee.

Wentworth pushed Susan in front of him, and kept on running, and the policeman aimed again. But just then a southbound express train came rushing toward them on the next track, and its powerful spotlight blinded the uniformed man. His shot went wild. And by the time he got the light out of his eyes and was ready to fire again, Wentworth had reached the station, and had boosted Susan up onto the platform.

The ticket agent in the booth stared at them as if they were mad, as they raced through the turnstiles and up the stairs to the street. It brought them out halfway around Columbus Circle from the Steel Building, and they could see that a vast mob of people had gathered in the street to watch the raid on the Mandalay Gardens. The crowds overflowed into the gutters all around, and the press was so thick that it was difficult to get through.

But no one paid the slightest attention to the puffy faced man in the tan suit, and the slim girl in what seemed to be a purple raincoat which wiggled their way through the crowd toward Broadway. Once, Wentworth looked back, and saw the pursuing policeman standing at the mouth of the subway kiosk, scratching his head in perplexity. He must have realized that his quarry was lost in such a crowd.

A moment later Wentworth hailed a cab on Broadway, and they were speeding toward the East End apartment.

NITA KEPT a complete change of wardrobe in each of

122

Wentworth's retreats, in the event of emergency. And from these he told Susan to select whatever clothes might fit her, though Nita was taller. Susan found a blouse and skirt which she thought would do, and she handed the cloak out to him over the dressing screen.

Wentworth left her then, and hurried to his own room. He quickly discarded the personality and the clothes of Joe Moulton, and became once more Richard Wentworth. As he worked over his facial details, his mind flew back and forth, from possibility to possibility. He could see no way out. With Nita in the hands of Red Feather, Wentworth could do nothing but bow in defeat. He understood too well, now, how Irene Blount must have felt when she almost brought herself to commit murder to save her daughter from torture. And how Arnold Metz had felt when he deliberately made a thief of himself for Susan's sake.

What, he asked himself, would he—Wentworth—not do to preserve Nita from the fate of Ellen Blount? Suppose Red Feather demanded that he commit a crime? Could he refuse, knowing that Nita would suffer unspeakable tortures while he smugly refused to demean himself?

No! Anything that Red Feather asked, he must be prepared to do! And even as the full force of that realization struck him, the phone rang!

The phone in this East End Avenue apartment was hooked up on a party line with the phone in his officially listed residence, which was only a block away. So that when it rang there he had only to pick it up here to answer it.

For a long minute he stood over that phone, debating whether to answer it. Out of a sure instinct as well as knowledge of how the criminal mind operates, he was certain that this was Red Feather, calling to lay down an ultimatum. If he should fail to answer it, the time of Nita's ordeal might be delayed. He might have more time to track down Red Feather and his organization.

Yet he could not bring himself to ignore that call. Within him there was a terrible turmoil and impatience. He must know the worst at once. *He must answer now!*

Before picking up the instrument, however, he took some elementary precautions. He picked up another phone and dialed the Telephone Company Emergency office. Giving his name, he requested tersely that the call coming in on the other line be traced. His connection with Commissioner Kirkpatrick was known to the company officials, and they asked no unnecessary questions. He hung up, and switched on the photoelectric recording device, which would make a record of the caller's voice, thus enabling him to analyze the tone content for future use.

The phone was still ringing when he picked it up.

"Wentworth speaking," he said curtly.

That same cold, emotionless voice snapped at his eardrums.

"You know, of course, who this is, Wentworth?"

"No."

"Then shall we say… Red Feather?"

A COLD rage gripped Wentworth, but he kept his voice level. "What do you want, Red Feather?"

"My dear Wentworth! From you there is only one thing I want; a little service which I should like you to perform for me.

I am certain that you will gladly do it—when you learn that your lovely Nita is—er—a guest of mine."

"How do I know that's true?"

As he asked the last question, a light flashed in front of the desk, indicating that there was a call on the other phone. He picked it up with his left hand, and whispered, "Wentworth talking."

"Telephone Company, Mr. Wentworth. That call is coming from a drug store pay station at Two Hundred and Forty-Second Street and Broadway—"

"Police!" he said into the phone, and hung up.

At his other ear, the voice of Red Feather was speaking unctuously: "... so if you require proof that she is my guest, I shall be glad to send it to you. Shall we say—one of her fingers? Which finger would you prefer? The index finger is too valuable, of course. Perhaps you would like to see her thumb?"

"No," said Wentworth, restraining the rage that welled up within him. "I'll take your word for it."

"Ah, so! That is much better. Now we come to the thing which I wish you to do."

"If I do this thing, whatever it is, do you promise to set her free?"

"Hardly, Mr. Wentworth. Hardly. She is too pleasant a guest. I will only promise that life will not become—er—unbearable for her. You understand? You were at the Mandalay Gardens. You saw the body of Ellen Blount. You comprehend what I mean."

"You mean that if I do this thing, you won't torture her?"

"Exactly. And as I require other things of you, you will do

them. Should you fail me, then you will sentence your beautiful friend to a very hideous ordeal. In other words, you are virtually my servant."

Wentworth gripped the phone tightly—so tightly that his knuckles shone white. He wanted to keep Red Feather on the phone as long as possible. Yet he could hardly believe that the man was so foolish as to remain there long enough for the police to come.

"What is it that you want me to do?"

He tried to keep his voice steady.

"Your first task," said that implacable voice, "will be the murder of Commissioner Kirkpatrick!"

CHAPTER 13
SUSAN REMEMBERS
THE SUNSET

THOSE WORDS struck like individual hammer blows against Richard Wentworth's brain. A cold wave of hopelessness swept over him.

The devilish coldness of Red Feather's voice had not changed by so much as a single tonal wave while he voiced that mad, inhuman order. It was so unbelievable that he might have thought Red Feather was making some macabre joke, had he not remembered the case of Irene Blount. She, too, had been ordered to murder a man in order to save her daughter. Red Feather had wanted Wentworth dead. His men had failed in the attempt at the Mallard Hotel, so he had callously ordered Irene

Blount to do the job. And now that he had Wentworth under his thumb, he was going to force him to remove Kirkpatrick, who, as an efficient police commissioner, was dangerous to his fiendish operations.

Wentworth forced himself to speak in a normal tone of voice. If he could only keep that vicious devil on the phone a little longer, the police might get there and pick him up.

"What you ask," he said, "is quite impossible. Stanley Kirkpatrick is my friend—"

"You may have your choice, Wentworth," Red Feather interrupted. "Stanley Kirkpatrick, or Nita van Sloan. I assure you that Kirkpatrick's death at your hand will be a far easier one than Nita van Sloan's death—at *my* hand!"

Suddenly, a new sound came very clearly to Wentworth over the phone, as a sort of background to Red Feather's voice. It was the sound of stuttering machine-guns!

Wentworth's eyes glinted, and his whole body tautened. Without doubt, those were machine-guns. The police had arrived there then!

But that sudden hope died in his breast a moment later, when the immutable voice of Red Feather spoke again.

"I see that you have had my call traced, Wentworth. It is too bad. Unfortunately for the police, only one squad car has arrived. I took the precaution of planting a number of my men in the neighborhood. Those sounds you heard were machine-guns, all right. But they belong to *my* men. The police are quite dead, my dear Wentworth! I must be leaving now, before more police arrive. Goodbye, my dear Wentworth! It is now almost midnight. I give you until five o'clock in the morning to carry out my order concerning Commissioner Kirkpatrick. After five—if the Commissioner is still alive—you may pass the time imagining the screams of agony which your Nita will be uttering!"

The phone clicked in Wentworth's ear as Red Feather hung up.

White-faced, he flung away from the desk—to see little Susan Metz standing in the doorway.

She was clad in one of Nita's blouses, and a plaid skirt, which she had pinned up around her waist. She was staring at him with wide, frightened eyes.

"That—that was Red Feather?"

"Yes!" he said bitterly.

"He—he wants you to kill somebody?"

"Yes."

"He's holding someone you—love?"

"Yes."

"Oh!" There was such a wealth of sympathy in her young eyes as she came running to him, that he forced a smile for her.

"I don't know who you are," she said. "But believe me, I'm sorry for you if—if your sweetheart is a victim of Red Feather."

NITA VAN SLOAN

"My name is Wentworth," he told her gently. "This is my apartment."

"But," her face clouded with perplexity, "the Spider brought me here. I know who he is. He's a man in a brown suit—"

"The Spider phoned me to come here," Wentworth told her. "He said he had left you in my apartment. The Spider frequently makes use of my services. His orders are that I take you to your father. I know everything that has happened to you. The Spider instructed me to question your father, since he cannot go there himself. Perhaps your father can give us some lead to Red Feather."

She looked up trustingly at Wentworth. "If the Spider trusts you, then I will, too!" Then she added diffidently, "I—I hope you can save your sweetheart."

"Perhaps," Wentworth said tightly, "I shall have to do what Irene Blount did. But even that won't save Nita!"

IN FIFTEEN minutes they were at the rooming house around the corner from the Mallard Hotel, where Wentworth had left Metz, lulled to sleep by a hypodermic needle.

They ascended in the automatic elevator, and rang the bell. Jackson opened the door. He had come over as soon as it was safe to leave the Mallard.

Jackson was in his shirtsleeves, and he was sweating a little.

"I can't make him talk, sir," he said. "He's been conscious for an hour, but he won't open his mouth."

Wentworth motioned to Susan to remain outside, and he entered the room.

Metz was sitting up on the bed. His appearance was miserable. His clothes were rumpled, and there were deep bags under his eyes. His lips were trembling. Wentworth pulled a chair over to face him.

Metz put out a supplicating hand. "Please—have you got any news? Have there been any murders today? Any—any girls found—dead?"

"Yes," said Wentworth. He saw Metz stiffen, and a dreadful look of despair come into his face.

"Damn you all!" he shrieked. "You've murdered my daughter. If you'd let me give the money to Red Feather, she'd still be alive!"

"It wasn't your daughter, Metz. It was Ellen Blount. Susan is safe."

"*Safe?*" Metz's eyes opened wide.

Wentworth got up and opened the door. "Come in, Susan," he said.

He and Jackson stepped out in hall, so as not to witness the reunion between father and daughter. It would have been too painful for them.

While they waited out there, Wentworth swiftly told Jackson the story of the evening.

"Ram Singh is in the hospital—unconscious," he finished. "The doctors say he must have a heart of leather. The knife just scraped it. He'll be laid up for a month, but he'll live. But in the meantime, he's unconscious and Nita's in Red Feather's hands. Whatever they know, I'll never learn from them in time to stop Red Feather. So Jackson, I guess I'm at the end of my rope. At five o'clock in the morning, I've got to finish up—*kaput!* A shot in the brain will do it for me. But Nita—when will it end for her?"

JACKSON'S BIG hands were clenching and unclenching at his sides. "You can't do that, Major. You can't take your own life!"

He dropped his eyes before Wentworth's gaze. He knew that Wentworth could not live and remain sane, knowing the unspeakable agony which Nita would be enduring.

At last he thought of an argument. "You must live, sir! You must live to bring that fiend to book. We'll track him down, sir—"

Once more he stopped. He could read his master's mind.

With Nita gone, there would be no incentive for Wentworth to go on living—not even the incentive of vengeance; not even the Spider's loathing for crime.

Silently, the two men turned and reentered the room.

Susan and her father were sitting on the bed side by side, with hands entwined. Metz looked twenty years younger than he had looked fifteen minutes before. His eyes swept up to Wentworth, and they were filmed with gratitude.

"Red Feather would have killed Susan next, if the Spider hadn't broken up his plans. Susan tells me, Mr. Wentworth, that you are a friend of the Spider. If you can give the Spider a message, tell him that I shall return the money I stole, and take my punishment for it. I wish there was something I could do to repay the Spider—or *you*, who are his friend. I know that you are in trouble. If I could only help—"

Susan said, "I told dad about—about Nita. He wants to help you. But there's so little he knows."

Wentworth's face was bleak. "There's nothing you can tell me, then?"

METZ SHOOK his head miserably. "I never saw Red Feather. The only contact was made with me by phone, after Susan was kidnapped."

Wentworth turned to the girl. "What about you, Susan? How were you kidnapped? Did you see the men who did it?"

"I had phoned for a cab," she said. "I was going to visit a friend uptown. When the cab came to the house, I got into it. And suddenly, two of those brown men appeared from nowhere. They were dressed in street clothes. One of them put his hand over my mouth so I couldn't scream, and the other stuffed a chloroform sponge against my nose. The next thing I knew, I was alone in a little room with a barred window. The window was too high for me to look out—"

She broke off, startled, as there was a sudden rush of feet in the hall outside. Someone turned the knob and thrust the door in, violently—and Commissioner Stanley Kirkpatrick burst into the room, followed by half a dozen plainclothesmen.

Kirkpatrick's glance rested only for a second on Wentworth, and then flicked over to Metz.

"Arnold Metz," he said, "you are under arrest!"

Metz sighed. "I was about to give myself up."

Kirkpatrick snorted. "And you, Dick, are also under arrest—for harboring a fugitive from justice!"

"How did you find this place?" Wentworth asked.

The Commissioner nodded toward Detective Murdoch, who had come in behind him.

"Murdoch spotted you in a cab with this young woman. He tailed you, and then phoned me. "I'm sorry, Dick, but I've got to lock you up. There's a little explaining you'll have to do. The Spider escaped from us, over at the Mandalay Gardens. I'll want to know where you've been for the last two hours."

Detectives were putting handcuffs on Metz. He was standing with squared shoulders, his head held high. "I'm not afraid anymore!" he said.

Kirkpatrick nodded to Wentworth. "It's your turn, Dick—for the handcuffs." He motioned to another of the detectives.

"Wait, Kirk!" Wentworth said suddenly. "There's something I've got to tell you."

"Well?"

"Not here. In the hall."

KIRKPATRICK LOOKED at him suspiciously, then shrugged and led the way out into the hall. The door remained open so the detectives could watch them; but they couldn't hear what was said.

"All right, Dick," the Commissioner said. "What is it?"

"I have to be free now, Kirk. Nita's in trouble."

The Commissioner raised his eyebrows. "What do you mean?"

Wentworth lowered his voice. "Red Feather has her!"

"What!"

"He's going to put her to the torture at five o'clock this morning."

"By God, Dick!" exclaimed Stanley Kirkpatrick. "I can't believe it. I don't want to believe it. Has he made a demand on you?"

"Yes."

"Then do it. Do anything. But don't let the same thing happen to Nita that happened to Ellen Blount!"

Wentworth smiled wearily. "No, Kirk, I can't do what he asks."

"Well, what is it, man?" Kirkpatrick demanded. "Are you afraid to tell me?"

"Almost, Kirk. He wants me to—murder *you!*"

Kirkpatrick's face seemed to congeal. A long, low sigh escaped from his lips.

"Dick," he said slowly and distinctly, "if it's my life that will save Nita from the torture, you're welcome to it!"

Wentworth shook his head. "Just give me a chance to find her. Don't put obstacles in my way."

"All right, Dick. Whatever you say. I'll go further. If it should be necessary for the Spider to operate tonight, I'll give orders to my men not to molest him."

"Thanks, Kirk. If I can contact the Spider, I'll ask his help."

"And what's more, Dick, if the Spider catches up with Red Feather, I won't complain if the Spider takes the law into his own hands!"

The two men returned to the room, and Kirkpatrick waved aside the detective with the handcuffs. There was a look of terrible intensity in his eyes as he issued swift orders to be spread through the Department—a truce with the Spider—till five o'clock in the morning. Mr. Wentworth to receive full cooperation in whatever he required....

Susan Metz was comforting her father. "They won't keep you in prison long, dad. They can't. I need you. I'll be thinking of you all the time. Thinking of how you'll be looking out of the window with bars. And maybe the window will be too high for you, too, so all you can see is the mail plane as it flies north at sunset."

Richard Wentworth suddenly uttered a hoarse, wild cry. He thrust the detectives aside, and seized Susan by the arm, swinging her around violently.

"What about the mail plane at sunset?"

Susan winced from the pain of his steel grip on her arm. She looked up into his eyes, and suddenly she was breathless.

"The mail plane," she whispered. "I was in a cell for a week. Every night, just at sunset, it passed quite low, flying north. It had a green light on the right wing, and a red light on the left one. It was the only thing I could see from my window. The plane had a number on the wings which I made out once or twice in the twilight. It was NC451. Every night I tried to reach the window to wave my handkerchief, but it was no use. I couldn't reach the sill."

There was a bright, dancing light in the eyes of Richard Wentworth. He seized Susan about the waist, lifted her up high, and kissed her.

"Susan," he exclaimed, "you're the most gorgeous thing in the world!"

He set her down, and swung on Kirkpatrick. "Get it, Kirk?"

The Commissioner's eyes glittered. "Let's go!" he said. "We'll know what company owns that plane in fifteen minutes. Then we'll check every mail route the outfit operates!"

CHAPTER 14
RED FEATHER'S LAIR!

IT WAS a great, modern castle, set high on a cliff overlooking the Hudson River, and located just north of the boundary line of New York City. Five acres of landscaped grounds lay between the massive structure and the road. On the west there was the river. On the east, south and north there ran a tall stone wall, its upper surface encrusted with jagged bits of broken glass.

Twenty feet inside the stone wall there was a fence of barbed wire. Small, dead animals lay against that fence—animals twisted into grotesque contortions which could only have been achieved by the application of a powerful charge of electricity. In the twenty-foot wide space of no man's land between stone wall and electrically charged wire fence, there roamed three huge mastiffs, hungry and growling. They had been taught never to touch the wire.

From the tower of the castle, two brilliant searchlights played constantly upon the grounds, rotating in opposite circles, and moving at a speed calculated to light up each sector of the grounds every four minutes.

All these things Richard Wentworth observed carefully, and noted in his memory. Six times Jackson had driven up and down the road skirting the castle property, and Wentworth had lain prone on the roof of the car with a pair of field glasses glued to his eyes. By the end of the sixth trip, there was little he did not know about the dispositions against a surprise raid on the castle.

After a feverish hour in police headquarters, checking by phone with the air lines, they had found plane NC451, and had caught one of the plane's pilots in Albany, preparing for the return trip. Without hesitation, over the phone, he had given them the exact location of the place answering their description.

Susan Metz's story had given them enough to go on. It had to be a place set on a high cliff, because she had said that the planes flew low enough to distinguish the number. And surely, the pilot couldn't have failed to note barred windows.

So now they had the place. This was Red Feather's lair. Here—and the odds were a hundred to one in favor of the supposition—was where Nita, and perhaps many others, were being held for the unspeakable tortures which Red Feather evolved for them.

The next question had been one of jurisdiction. Being just beyond the City Line, Kirkpatrick had no authority to act. It was a question of calling in the County law officers, or the State Troopers.

In either case there would have to be an application for a search warrant, and a loss of valuable time. And even if a search warrant could have been obtained without delay, Wentworth argued that Red Feather would have means to dispose of his prisoners so that no trace could ever be found of them. For a man of Red Feather's devilish ingenuity would certainly make provision for the possibility of detection and raid. Just as he had provided a means of escape for his killers from the Mandalay Gardens, and just as he had arranged for protection while he made his phone call to Richard Wentworth, so surely would he have planned for the time when the law would come down upon him.

And so it was decided that Wentworth should go alone.

Kirkpatrick, at the conference with Captain Sheffield of the State Police, had put it a little differently.

"This," he had said, "is a case for the Spider. He is the only one man who could get in there without giving the alarm."

"Perhaps I could get in touch with the Spider," Wentworth had said tentatively.

And there they let it lie—except that Kirkpatrick obtained permission from Captain Sheffield to station a large squad of men on the City Line, with the understanding that if they noticed a disturbance which required their attention, they had permission to cross over. And as an added precaution, a police boat was hove to, just around the bend in the river, with a machine gun on the prow ready for action.

But it was Richard Wentworth who had to go in there.

SO WHEN all the observations had been made, the car made one more trip down the road, with all lights out. Halfway along the stone fence, it swerved in sharply, until it was almost touching the wall.

From the roof of the car, a black cloaked figure arose. It peered over the wall, waiting until the two moving searchlights had passed that spot. Then, working swiftly, the figure grasped the end of a wide board—a two-by-eight—which someone handed up from below. Swiftly, the cloaked man swung the board over the wall, sliding it out until one end of it rested on top of the barbed wire fence, and the near end remained on the stone wall. Thus, it made a perfect bridge over the twenty feet of no man's land.

It took almost the full four minutes to complete that operation. Then the cloaked figure dropped back to the roof of the car, waiting till the searchlights passed once more. As soon as they were gone, the cloaked figure called down softly, "Here goes, Jackson."

"Happy landings, Major!" was all that Jackson said.

And then the Spider was on the wall, and crawling on the eight inch bridge over the no man's land. He moved swiftly, yet surely. He must avoid falling into the jaws of the vicious mastiffs below, and he must also be across before the searchlights returned.

He reached the end of the plank and jumped to the ground inside the barbed wire fence just as the beam of the searchlight swung around to finger once more at the spot. Both beams met right at this point, which was why he had chosen it, for it gave him twice the time.

Now, as the light splashed across the ground, the Spider lay flat, with his black cloak billowing out about him. A watcher in the castle might note the dark splotch on the ground, and might also notice the plank. And if he should be seen, the Spider would have no knowledge of it until a vicious burst of machine-gun bullets cut him down, or perhaps, until one of the flamethrowers burned him to a crisp.

But it was a chance he must take. Behind him, Jackson was already pulling back the plank. It was useless as a means of escape, for it would be impossible to scale the barbed wire fence to reach it. The Spider's bridges were burned behind him!

And now, as he inched forward toward the castle across the smooth and velvety lawn, the three mastiffs in the twenty foot enclosure became aware of his presence, and began to utter low growls.

He paid no attention to them. He knew dogs. Their growls would grow in intensity as the strange man smell *approached* them, until they were barking loud enough to sound an alarm. But he was now moving *away* from them. Their growls would continue. But the dogs would not begin to bark.

Slowly, cautiously, he made his way across the lawn, watchful of pits or charged wires. Also, he must be careful to flatten out every four minutes, when the stark glare of the searchlights struck with their merciless light. The castle was still a hundred yards distant. He could not hope to traverse all that space without being detected. Red Feather had not worked out this elaborate system of protection without posting adequate guards. And a watchful guard could not help spotting the black blotch he made against the green grass. Yet, he must try every trick at his command. It must be time for Jackson to send up his rocket....

CHAPTER 15
BED OF PAIN

WITHIN THE great castle there was an air of watchful expectancy.

The Baron Cornelius Crispi sat in a stiff-backed chair in a chamber on the ground floor. His chair faced the open French windows. He had a pair of field glasses glued to his eyes, and the glasses were trained upon a dark blotch that moved slowly and laboriously across the green grass.

The Baron Cornelius Crispi chuckled.

"A very ingenious fellow, this Spider!" he said.

On the Baron's right side stood a small brown Hindu with an automatic rifle. On his left stood another Hindu with a flamethrower. Both were watching the dark splotch on the grass. But it was to neither of these that the Baron Crispi talked. He was addressing himself to someone in the rear of the room.

Since the entire chamber was in darkness, it was difficult for anyone whose eyes had not become accustomed the gloom to discern just how that rear half was equipped.

But, as one's eyes gradually adjusted themselves, they would have widened at the ghastly sight presented to them.

The entire rear half was occupied by a sinister machine which at first sight was reminiscent of the horrible days of the Inquisition, in the dark Middle Ages when men like Torquemada devoted their lives to the scientific study of the most effective means of producing pain and suffering in the human body.

Psychologists of the abnormal in human behavior maintain that the streak of sadism—the desire to inflict pain on others—which was so pronounced in the dark eras of human history, has not been eradicated from human consciousness by the refinements of civilization, but that it is merely dormant, ready to come to the fore whenever opportunity presents.

The ghastly machine* in the room behind Baron Crispi was definite proof in support of this theory.

The backbone of the machine consisted of a bed of spikes, whose points were ground to a deadly sharpness. Suspended eight inches above the spikes, was a woman. She was tied firmly by the ankles. But at the other end she had no support except

---

* AUTHOR'S NOTE: This machine has been faithfully reproduced on the cover by our artist.

that which she could furnish for herself by gripping two ropes hanging over her head. She had to support the entire weight of her body by her hold upon those ropes. Each time that she weakened, her body would drop and the deadly sharp spikes would bite into her back. If she let go entirely, her weight would drive her body down upon those spikes and she would die slowly and agonizingly, impaled by her own weight.

Nita van Sloan was thankful that it was dark, so that the agony written upon her face could not be witnessed by Baron Cornelius Crispi. She had been suspended over that bed of spikes for twenty minutes now, and the strain upon *every* muscle of her lithe body was almost unbearable. Already, she was tempted to let go, and give up the struggle for life. But she knew that even this would not be the end. It would take her hours and hours to die, and the Baron would sit and gloat, and watch, and keep rhythmic time to her death struggles with his tapping, patent leather shoe.

Directly above her head there was another threat—a guillotine of spikes, sliding up and down in grooved channels. The guillotine hung in such a position that if it dropped, it would pierce her throat, but not at the jugular vein. She would bleed to death slowly and surely.

The rope that controlled this guillotine ran across the room and was tied to the arm of Baron Crispi's chair.

"This, my dear," he explained to her," is to take care of any emergency—such as the Spider's unexpected arrival. Even if he should succeed in entering and overpowering my guards, I would have only to slash the ropes with this knife, and you would die before his very eyes!"

"Why do you hate him so much?" Nita gasped.

"Why?" Crispi laughed harshly. "The Spider has blocked me everywhere tonight—or, rather, last night. He snatched Metz from right under my nose, with two hundred thousand dollars in cash. Then he caused me a loss of almost a quarter of a million in money and jewels when he interrupted the holdup at the Mandalay Gardens. He killed Blagg, one of my best men. And he brought Susan Metz back to her father, thus depriving me of my hold over that man!"

CRISPI STOPPED talking, growled deep in his throat like a terrier from which someone has taken a luscious bone. "You, my dear, are paying for the Spider's achievements!"

Nita had no more strength to talk. Every last drop of her strength was required to keep her from slipping down upon the pointed spikes.

Crispi was talking now, low and vehemently. "There is no one in the world today who can appreciate the monetary value of human suffering—no one but myself. Motion picture producers, actors, writers, publishers, all try to make fortunes catering to the whims and desires of the multitude. But they all forget that there is a stronger instinct in the human race than the desire for pleasures—the instinct to avoid pain!

"Look at a baby. If it is burned, it will never touch fire again. Look at the millions of invalids who spend their last penny for doctors to relieve them of pain. Therefore I—Baron Cornelius Crispi—have devised the plan of profiting by the instinct to avoid pain. People will pay huge sums frantically, to be spared pain and torture. Even you, my dear, would give me anything I asked of you, in order to be spared this agony!"

From his chair he regarded her sardonically. "Well now, my dear, speak up. Suppose I were to release you—at the price of betraying the Spider into my hands. Suppose I were to lift you off at this very moment, and relieve the terrible strain upon all the muscles of your body—*would you help me trap the Spider?*"

Nita was gasping with the dreadful exertion. But she drew in a deep breath, and managed to say in a fairly even tone, "If I weren't a lady, I would tell you to go to hell!"

Crispi spat out a curse, and flung violently away from her. "A little while longer, my dear—you will be pleading with me. The longest anyone has lasted over those spikes was an hour and a half! But, if I am correct in my observations, I will trap the Spider without your aid!"

For ten minutes the Baron watched the movements of that dark shadow on the lawn. He felt secure with his Hindu killers at his side, and the rope which controlled the guillotine tied to his chair. He was ready to slash at the rope at an instant's notice. As he watched, he took grim pleasure in telling Nita everything that he observed.

And it was more the fear for Wentworth than for herself which caused her to strain at the ropes. For she knew Dick Wentworth; she knew that he was coming here, hoping that if he couldn't free her, he might die with her. Otherwise, why would he enter so boldly?

The Spider picked up a scimitar and swung to meet the vicious attack of Baron Crispi...

"Ah!" Crispi was saying, with his eyes at the binoculars. "Your Spider is moving again! Inch by inch!"

He turned to the Hindu at his left—the one with the automatic rifle. "We shall try to capture him alive, Mali, if possible. There are some—er—experiments I should like to try upon this mighty Spider! Besides—he is fabulously rich."

In silence they waited, watching the progress of that shadowy figure.

"See," said Crispi, "how clever he thinks he is! He has reached a tree. He stands erect, thinking that he is safe in its shadow—" He broke off, uttering an exclamation of annoyance.

In the distance to the left, a rocket suddenly went soaring up to the sky. It spread into a multicolored band of light, and then dissolved high in the heavens.

Crispi watched, frowning. "Perhaps that is a signal, Mali. Perhaps he does not come alone after all. If police come, we must have everything ready, Mali. All the prisoners go in the underground chambers—including Miss van Sloan. Our torture machines will then be merely specimens—eh, Mali?"

He chuckled in that slimy, gloating way of his. "We have foreseen everything, Miss van Sloan. Please give up thought of rescue. Let us see what your friend the Spider is doing. Perhaps that rocket had no connection with him…."

He swung the glasses back to the tree, and clucked with satisfaction. "He has not moved yet. How long does he think to wait? If he knew that you, my dear, were tearing the muscles of your body to keep off those spikes, perhaps he would hurry!"

Nita was wondering how close Dick was. If she used every

remaining bit of strength to shout a warning to him, would he hear it? After such a shout, she would be too weak to hold herself up. She would have to let go and drop on the spikes. She'd do it, too, if she could only be sure it would save him. But to waste that precious energy, and not have him hear her cry….

Dear God! What was that shadow above her?

Was it a shadow, or were her eyes playing tricks on her? Maybe, in her weakness, she only imagined that shadowy….

But no. Surely, those were eyes peering down into the room through the trapdoor which housed the guillotine frame. Yes… something seemed to be drifting down toward her!

Hope! Hope began to surge in her breast, and then died instantly. For Crispi, with the glasses still at his eyes, was saying, "Your Spider has not moved for a long time, my dear. I think I will make you scream. That will hurry him!"

Crispi got up from his chair, moved over toward Nita. Mali came with him. The other Hindu remained to watch from the window. Crispi clapped his hands and a small group of white turbaned Hindus appeared armed with gleaming scimitars.

"You will go out on the grounds," he told them. "Watch the fool who hides by that tree. When the girl screams, he will move. Then close in on him. Wound him, but do not kill him. And bring him here!"

He nodded to one of the Hindus. "Slash her across the stomach, Vodee. One slash—enough to make her scream."

Vodee licked his lips and raised the scimitar in one hand. With the other he reached to Nita's dress.

But before he could touch her, the black and sinister figure

149

of the Spider hurtled down upon him from the trapdoor above, and the Spider's feet, lashing out, smashed the Hindu's jaw as if it had been made of china. Vodee catapulted backward, and the Spider swung past through the air, like a man on a trapeze.

He was swinging from a line of Web, which he had tied about his waist to give him freedom of action with both hands.

The Spider had outmaneuvered Crispi!

He had brought an extra cloak and hat into the grounds with him. And when Jackson had released the flare, the Spider had taken advantage of the momentary distraction of those in the house to drape the cloak and hat on a branch. Then he himself had stolen across the lawn and climbed the creeping ivy to the second floor window, whence he had come down into this chamber of torture.

Baron Crispi realized this in a flash, as the Spider swung free after smashing Vodee's jaw. He shrieked orders to his Hindus, and they came trooping back from the grounds with flashing scimitars, while Mali trained his automatic rifle upon the flying figure.

But the Spider's guns were already belching. Mali went down with a slug through his own belly, and the other Hindu with the flamethrower took the blasting lead from the Spider's gun square in his face.

BARON CRISPI uttered a cry of rage and sprang across to his chair, snatching up the knife with which to cut the rope that would send the spiked guillotine down upon Nita's throat.

The Spider, swinging free above her, was unable to get a shot at Crispi, because of the heavy oak chair. His quick mind grasped the meaning of the rope running from the guillotine slide to the Baron's chair. He sent himself swinging back, shouting to Nita, *"Hang on, girl!"*

His foot smashed another of the Hindus out of the way, and he reached the guillotine slide just as Crispi cut the rope. The spikes began to drop toward Nita's throat, and Wentworth thrust out one of his guns. As the slide dropped in the smooth grooves, he placed the muzzle against the frame and fired six times!

The impact of those heavy forty-five caliber slugs, striking with the impact weight of a fifty pound sledgehammer, twisted the metal frame of the groove. The heavy blade jammed to a stop in mid-descent!

Baron Crispi screamed with rage and snatched up a revolver. The Hindus dashed in, the nearest one of them trying to slash at the ropes by which Nita was supporting herself.

One of the Spider's guns was empty now. He threw it away, and smashed a terrific left into the jaw of the Hindu who was trying to cut the ropes. The man went flying backward, his head cocked at an unnatural angle.

Now lead was whining past the Spider, converging upon him from Crispi's gun as well as from the guns of the Hindus.

The Spider, in his black cloak and hat, was a poor target for them, but his own shooting was uncannily accurate. He had only one gun, and he must make every shot count. The narrow confines of that torture chamber were filled with the fumes of cordite and the thunder of heavy explosions as he blasted again and again at the advancing Hindus. Four of them fell in as many seconds, and the others had had enough. They turned and fled, leaving their dead and wounded on the floor.

Nita had managed to wind the ropes about her wrists for greater purchase. She was watching the fight with blazing eyes, forgetful of her own predicament.

She screamed. "Look out, Dick! Behind you!"

The Spider, still swinging from his Web, kicked away instinctively from the framework, sending his body swinging outward. It was Nita's warning and his swift action which saved his life, for Baron Crispi was kneeling on one knee and taking careful aim with a long barreled Luger. He fired just as Wentworth kicked away, and the bullet smashed harmlessly into the framework of the torture machine. The Baron's face became a gaunt, malevolent visage of hatred as he aimed a second time.

The Spider's gun was empty.

But he was not at the end of his resources. The Hindu whom he had kicked in the jaw had dropped his scimitar across Nita's stomach. The Spider grasped and hurled it, and the blade cut diagonally into Crispi's forehead, a fraction of a second before he fired. His shot missed the Spider, and he fell backward with blood streaming from a shallow hole in his forehead. It was not fatal, but blood blinded him momentarily.

The Spider acted now with the speed of a fighting man who knows that a split-second may mean the difference between life and death.

His fingers slipped to his waist, loosening the noose which he had looped about himself. With one hand he supported himself by reaching for the line of Web above him, while with the other he slipped the loosened noose down until it dropped from his legs.

He was now hanging by one arm, directly above Nita, who was showing signs of weakening. She was gasping for breath. Looking down at her Wentworth saw that her whole body was trembling with the strain.

"Another minute, Nita!" he called, and hurled himself past her body, letting go of the Web just as he acquired momentum.

Crispi had wiped the blood from his eyes and he was leveling the Luger again when Wentworth's hurtling weight struck him in the chest. The smashing impact flung him backward. His head struck the heavy back of the oak chair and he collapsed.

THE SPIDER wasted not even a second glance at him. He snatched up a scimitar and slashed at the ropes binding Nita's ankles to the framework. In a moment he had her off that terrible bed of spikes. Anyone else but Nita van Sloan would have collapsed, probably gone into a fit of hysterics. But not Nita.

She came into his arms swiftly, but her first words were, "Dick! There are other prisoners in this house—fifteen of them. Women, girls, and children whose loved ones that fiend has been forcing to commit hideous crimes by threatening torture to the prisoners. We must free them!"

The Spider nodded. "Come—"

He broke off as he glimpsed the look of horror in Nita's eyes. Sensing the danger behind him, he thrust her out of the way and swung to meet the vicious attack of Baron Cornelius Crispi, who had picked up one of the scimitars, and was coming at Wentworth with the blade raised high for a decapitating blow!

There was a wicked glint of triumph in Crispi's eyes. He was only three feet from the Spider, and the Spider was unarmed. The scimitar was coming around now in that vicious slash which would sever the Spider's head from his body!

The Spider's laughter clashed through the room. He dropped backward before the vicious onslaught, hitting the floor on his back just as Crispi slashed. The Barron's attack brought him forward at great momentum, and the Spider's legs rose straight in the air to catch Crispi, in the stomach. Crispi's forward charge carried him high up, riding on the Spider's feet. He described a parabola in the air, and sailed—straight for the bed of spikes in the torture machine!

A weird, dreadful cry pulsed from his throat. This inhuman student of human suffering couldn't take it when it was his turn.

The scream of fear turned to a gurgling rattle of animal fright as his body landed on the sharp tipped spikes. His weight and his momentum carried him far down upon those deadly points, and the *squoosh* of the barbs piercing bone and flesh and muscle was terrible to hear.

Crispi flailed about in agony for a half minute, his arms thrashing wildly, serving only to drive the spikes deeper.

"Mercy! Mercy..." he frothed. And then the finger of Mercy touched him. For one of those spikes had evidently driven to his heart. His body stiffened into dreadful rigidity. His mouth opened wide in one last attempt to scream... and he died!

Nita van Sloan turned her face away. And the Spider put an arm about her waist and led her out of that chamber of pain and terror....

THE SPIDER AND THE PAIN MASTER

TWENTY MINUTES later, Richard Wentworth—without his Spider makeup—led a staggering, pitiful group of women, girls and children out of that gray, grim castle to freedom. Nita van Sloan was on his arm as he greeted Commissioner Kirkpatrick who was standing with a squad of police at the gate.

"Glory be!" Kirkpatrick said. "We caught half a dozen Hindus escaping, and we came to see if you were still alive!

Wentworth nodded soberly. "And a monster is dead."

"You killed him?" Kirkpatrick demanded. "You killed Red Feather?"

Wentworth and Nita both exchanged looks.

"Why no, Kirk," said Wentworth." Not I. The Spider killed him. You know, it was the Spider who saved us all."

Commissioner Kirkpatrick scowled and shook his head. "The Spider deserves the thanks of thousands for what he did tonight, Dick. But I warn you—if the Spider walks again, I'll come down on him with the full force of the law! And that's a promise!"

Richard Wentworth shrugged without answering, and turned back to Nita. And she, looking into the depths of his eyes, knew that he was thinking of those who had died so terribly today, and also of those who were miraculously alive, and happy, and freed forever of the menace of Red Feather. And she swallowed the lump in her throat, and her long, patrician fingers touched his sleeve.

"I'm glad, Dick," she whispered throatily, "glad that the Spider walked again tonight!"

POPULAR HERO PULPS AVAILABLE NOW:

ACE G-MAN
- ❏ #1: The Suicide Squad Reports for Death — $14.95
- ❏ #2: Coffins for the Suicide Squad — $14.95
- ❏ #3: Shells for the Suicide Squad — $14.95
- ❏ #4: The Suicide Squad in Corpse-Town — $14.95
- ❏ #5: Wanted—In Three Pine Coffins — $14.95
- ❏ #6: The Suicide Squad's Dawn Patrol — $14.95
- ❏ #7: Targets for the Flaming Arrow — $16.95

OPERATOR 5
- ❏ #1: The Masked Invasion — $13.95
- ❏ #2: The Invisible Empire — $13.95
- ❏ #3: The Yellow Scourge — $13.95
- ❏ #4: The Melting Death — $13.95
- ❏ #5: Cavern of the Damned — $13.95
- ❏ #6: Master of Broken Men — $13.95
- ❏ #7: Invasion of the Dark Legions — $13.95
- ❏ #8: The Green Death Mists — $13.95
- ❏ #9: Legions of Starvation — $13.95
- ❏ #10: The Red Invader — $13.95
- ❏ #11: The League of War-Monsters — $13.95
- ❏ #12: The Army of the Dead — $13.95
- ❏ #13: March of the Flame Marauders — $13.95
- ❏ #14: Blood Reign of the Dictator — $13.95
- ❏ #15: Invasion of the Yellow Warlords — $13.95
- ❏ #16: Legions of the Death Master — $13.95
- ❏ #17: Hosts of the Flaming Death — $13.95
- ❏ #18: Invasion of the Crimson Death Cult — $13.95
- ❏ #19: Attack of the Blizzard Men — $13.95
- ❏ #20: Scourge of the Invisible Death — $13.95
- ❏ #21: Raiders of the Red Death — $13.95
- ❏ #22: War-Dogs of the Green Destroyer — $13.95
- ❏ #23: Rockets From Hell — $13.95
- ❏ #24: War-Masters from the Orient — $13.95
- ❏ #25: Crime's Reign of Terror — $13.95
- ❏ #26: Death's Ragged Army — $13.95
- ❏ #27: Patriots' Death Battalion — $13.95
- ❏ #28: The Bloody Forty-five Days — $13.95
- ❏ #29: America's Plague Battalions — $13.95
- ❏ #30: Liberty's Suicide Legions — $13.95
- ❏ #31: Siege of the Thousand Patriots — $13.95
- ❏ #32: Patriots' Death March — $14.95
- ❏ #33: Revolt of the Lost Legions — $14.95
- ❏ #34: Drums of Destruction — $14.95
- ❏ #35: The Army Without a Country — $14.95
- ❏ #36: The Bloody Frontiers — $14.95
- ❏ #37: The Coming of the Mongol Hordes — $14.95
- ❏ #38: The Siege That Brought Black Death — $16.95
- ❏ #39: Revolt of the Devil Men — $16.95
- ❏ #40: The Suicide Battalion — $16.95
- ❏ #41: The Day of the Damned — $16.95
- ❏ **NEW:** #42: The Dawn That Shook the World — $16.95

RED FINGER
- ❏ #1: Second-Hand Death — $24.95

G-8 AND HIS BATTLE ACES
- ❏ #1: The Bat Staffel — $13.95

CAPTAIN COMBAT
- ❏ #1: The Sky Beast of Berlin — $13.95
- ❏ #2: Red Wings For the Blood Battalion — $13.95
- ❏ #3: Low Ceiling For Nazi Hell Hawks — $13.95

DUSTY AYRES AND HIS BATTLE BIRDS
- ❏ #1: Black Lightning! — $13.95
- ❏ #2: Crimson Doom — $13.95
- ❏ #3: The Purple Tornado — $13.95
- ❏ #4: The Screaming Eye — $13.95
- ❏ #5: The Green Thunderbolt — $13.95
- ❏ #6: The Red Destroyer — $13.95
- ❏ #7: The White Death — $13.95
- ❏ #8: The Black Avenger — $13.95
- ❏ #9: The Silver Typhoon — $13.95
- ❏ #10: The Troposphere F-S — $13.95
- ❏ #11: The Blue Cyclone — $13.95
- ❏ #12: The Tesla Raiders — $13.95

MAVERICKS
- ❏ #1: Five Against the Law — $12.95
- ❏ #2: Mesquite Manhunters — $12.95
- ❏ #3: Bait for the Lobo Pack — $12.95
- ❏ #4: Doc Grimson's Outlaw Posse — $12.95
- ❏ #5: Charlie Parr's Gunsmoke Cure — $12.95

THE MYSTERIOUS WU FANG
- ❏ #1: The Case of the Six Coffins — $12.95
- ❏ #2: The Case of the Scarlet Feather — $12.95
- ❏ #3: The Case of the Yellow Mask — $12.95
- ❏ #4: The Case of the Suicide Tomb — $12.95
- ❏ #5: The Case of the Green Death — $12.95
- ❏ #6: The Case of the Black Lotus — $12.95
- ❏ #7: The Case of the Hidden Scourge — $12.95

THE SECRET 6
- ❏ #1: The Red Shadow — $13.95
- ❏ #2: House of Walking Corpses — $13.95
- ❏ #3: The Monster Murders — $13.95
- ❏ #4: The Golden Alligator — $13.95

CAPTAIN ZERO
- ❏ #1: City of Deadly Sleep — $13.95
- ❏ #2: The Mark of Zero! — $13.95
- ❏ #3: The Golden Murder Syndicate — $13.95